Fifth Formers at St Clare's

This is the sixth book
in the St Clare's school series

Published by Granada Publishing Limited in 1967
Reprinted 1968, 1969, 1970, 1971, 1972, 1974, 1975,
1976 (twice), 1977, 1978, 1979, 1980 (twice), 1982, 1983

ISBN 0 583 30065 0

First published in Great Britain by
Methuen & Co Ltd 1945
Copyright © Enid Blyton 1945

Granada Publishing Limited
Frogmore, St Albans, Herts AL2 2NF
and
36 Golden Square, London W1R 4AH
515 Madison Avenue, New York, NY 10022, USA
117 York Street, Sydney, NSW 2000, Australia
60 International Blvd, Rexdale, Ontario, R9W 6J2, Canada
61 Beach Road, Auckland, New Zealand

Printed and bound in Great Britain by
Cox & Wyman Ltd, Reading
Set in Times

Granada ®
Granada Publishing ®

Enid Blyton

Fifth Formers at St Clare's

A DRAGON BOOK

GRANADA

London Toronto Sydney New York

In the cupboard lay little Jane Teal

Back for the Winter Term

St. Clare's had stood silent and empty during eight weeks of the summer holiday. Except for the sound of mops and brushes, and a tradesman ringing at the bell, the place had been very quiet. The school cat missed the girls and wandered about miserably for the first week or two.

But now everything was different. The school coaches were rolling up the hill, full of chattering, laughing children – St. Clare's was beginning a new winter term!

"Who would think this was a winter term?" said Pat O'Sullivan, to her twin, Isabel. "The sun is as hot as it was in the summer. We might be able to have a few games of tennis, still."

"I shall certainly have a swim in the pool," said Bobby Ellis, whose face seemed even more freckled than usual. "I hope there's fresh water in today – I might have a swim after tea."

"Ah, you Bobbee! Always you must play tennis or swim or run or jump!" said Claudine, the little French girl. "And your freckles! Never did I see so many on one face. I have been careful in the hot sun these holidays – not one freckle did I catch!"

The girls laughed. Claudine was always terrified of getting freckles – but never did one appear on her pale face and white hands.

The girls poured into the school, running up the familiar steps, shouting to one another, dumping their lacrosse sticks everywhere.

"Hallo, Hilary! Hallo, Janet! Oh, there's Carlotta, looking more like a gypsy than ever. Hey, Carlotta, where did you go for your holidays? You look as dark as a gypsy."

"I have been to Spain," said Carlotta. "Some of my people live there, you know. I had a grand time."

5

"There's Mirabel – golly, she's awfully tall now!" said Isabel. "Gladys looks more like a mouse than ever beside her."

"Hallo!" said the big, strapping Mirabel, coming up. "How's every one?"

"Hallo, Mirabel, hallo Gladys," said the girls. "You've been spending the hols. together, haven't you? I bet you played tennis and swam all the time!"

Both Mirabel and Gladys were fond of games, and this term Mirabel was anxious to be sports captain at St. Clare's. She had been in the fifth form for two terms, and Annie Thomas, the sports captain, had let Mirabel help her. Now Annie had left, and there was a chance that Mirabel might be captain, for there was no one in the sixth form really fitted to have that post.

"Let's go and look at our classroom," said Bobby Ellis. "It was going to be re-decorated in the hols., I know. Let's see what it's like."

They all trooped upstairs to the big fifth form-room. Certainly it looked very nice, painted a pale banana yellow. The light was clean and clear in the room, and the view from the windows a lovely one.

"We've only got this term here – and then we go up into the sixth form!" said Hilary. "Fancy being at the top of the school! I remember when I first came to St. Clare's, I thought the fifth and sixth formers were almost grown-up. I hardly dared to speak to them."

"I expect the young ones think the same thing of us," said Janet. "I know most of them scuttle out of my way when I come along – like frightened rabbits!"

"I have a young sister in the second form this term," said Claudine, the French girl. "She came over with me from France. Look – there she is, the little Antoinette."

The girls looked out of the window. They saw a girl of about fourteen, very like the pale-faced, dark-haired Claudine, standing watching the others. She looked very self-possessed.

"Don't you want to go down and show Antoinette round a bit?" said Pat. "I bet she feels lonely and new."

"Ah, Antoinette would never feel so," said Claudine. "She can stand on her own toes, like me."

"Stand on her own feet, you mean," said Bobby, with a chuckle. "You'll never get those English sayings right, Claudine. Ah – there's old Mam'zelle!"

The girls watched Mam'zelle going out into the garden, an anxious look on her face.

"She is looking for the little Antoinette," said Claudine. "She has not seen her for two years. Ah, Antoinette will now be swamped in love and affection! My aunt will think her little niece Antoinette is as wonderful as me, her niece Claudine!"

Mam'zelle was Claudine's aunt, and this fact was at times useful to Claudine, and at other times, embarrassing. For Antionette just then it was most embarrassing. The little French girl had been enjoying herself, watching the excited English girls catching hold of one another's arms, swinging each other round, chasing one another, and generally behaving in the usual school-girl way – a way, however, that the demure Antoinette had not been used to.

Then, quite suddenly, an avalanche descended upon her, two plump arms almost strangled her, and a loud and excited voice poured out French endearments in first one ear and then another. Loud kisses were smacked on each cheek, and then another hug came which made Antoinette gasp for breath.

"Ah, *la petite* Antoinette, *mon petit chou*," cried Mam'zelle at the top of her voice. All the girls stopped playing and stared at Antoinette and Mam'zelle. They giggled. It was plain that Antoinette was not at all pleased to be greeted in public in this way. She disentangled herself as best she could.

She caught sight of her elder sister, Claudine, leaning out of a high window, grinning in delight. She pointed up to her at once.

"Dear *Tante* Mathilde, there is my sister Claudine who

7

looks for you. Now that she has seen you greet me, she will wish you to greet her too."

Mam'zelle glanced up and saw Claudine. Still holding Antoinette, she waved frantically and blew kisses. "Ah, there is the little Claudine too! Claudine, I come to embrace you."

Antoinette wriggled away and lost herself in the nearby crowd of girls. Mam'zelle turned her steps towards the door that led to the stairs. "I come, I come!" she called to Claudine.

"And I go," said Claudine, pushing away the giggling girls. "Mam'zelle will be quite overcome this term with *two* nieces here."

So, when poor Mam'zelle panted into the fifth-form classroom to embrace her second niece, Claudine was not to be found. "I have missed her, but I will find her!" cried Mam'zelle, and she beamed round at the fifth formers there.

"Ah, Bobbee, you have come back – and you Angela – and Alison – all of you, the dear girls! And you are going to work hard for me this term, so hard – for is it not next term that you go up into the top form, the sixth form. That is indeed a solemn thought!"

The French teacher went out of the room, hunting for her dear Claudine. The girls laughed. "Dear old Mam'zelle," said Hilary, "I shall never forget her, if I live to be a hundred! The tricks we've played on her – do you remember those awful stink-balls you had, Janet, when we were in the fourth form? I laughed till I cried then, when I saw Mam'-zelle's face as the smell reached her."

"There's only one new girl this term," said Janet, "in our form, I mean. I saw her name on the list downstairs. She's called Anne-Marie Longden. And Felicity Ray has come up from the fourth form."

"About time too," said Mirabel. "She's older than most of the fifth already. I think she's a bit batty."

"No, she's not – it's only that she's a real musical genius," said Gladys. "You've said yourself heaps of times that she is, Mirabel. She doesn't seem to care about anything but music – other lessons just roll off her, like water off a duck's back. She's always bottom of everything except music."

"Well, Miss Cornwallis won't be very thrilled if Felicity takes no notice of anything but music," said Bobby, who had reason to know that the fifth-form mistress was what the girls called among themselves "a real slave-driver". "I bet Felicity will know more geography, history and maths. this term than she has ever known all the time she has been at school!"

"Any other girls?" said Mirabel.

"Well, it's funny, Alma Pudden's name was down on the list of fifth formers," said Janet. "But she's sixth form, isn't she? I mean, when she came last term, she was put into the sixth form – but now her name is down for our form. Perhaps she's been put back into the fifth for some reason."

"Well, I wish she wasn't," said Bobby. "I can't say she thrills me. She's so like her name – puddeny! She's a bit like a suet pudding, fat and stodgy and dull."

"She's got a beastly temper," said Hilary. "I guess she won't be too pleased at coming down into the fifth form!"

Matron appeared at the door of the classroom with a tall, slender, dark-eyed girl, whose pale blonde hair made her eyes seem very black indeed.

"Hallo, fifth formers!" she said, her cheerful smile beaming at every one. "All back? Good girls. Now don't any of you dare to go down with mumps or measles, chicken pox or anything else! I've brought you the only new girl for your form – Anne-Marie Longden."

Anne-Marie smiled nervously. She was not pretty, but her golden hair and dark eyes made her rather striking. "Hallo," she said, awkwardly, "are you all fifth formers? What are your names?"

Hilary, who was head of the form, introduced every one quickly.

"These are the O'Sullivan twins, Pat and Isabel. You'll probably know t'other from which in a few terms! This is Janet, and this is Roberta, commonly called Bobby. You'll

9

always know her by her freckles! Look out for those two, for they know more tricks than any one else."

Anne-Marie smiled politely. Hilary went on, dragging first one girl forward and then another.

"This is Doris – she can mimic any one under the sun. She'll be mimicking *you* before long, Anne-Marie!"

Anne-Marie did not look as if this thrilled her very much. She thought Doris looked a rather clumsy, stupid girl. She did not see the intelligent eyes and humorous mouth of the born actress that Doris was.

"Here's Carlotta, dark as a gypsy!" went on Hilary. Carlotta gave her usual cheeky grin.

"And please let me tell you, Anne-Marie, that I was once a circus-girl, and rode horses in a circus ring," said Carlotta. "Angela is sure to tell you that sooner or later, so I may as well tell you now!"

The golden-haired beautiful girl called Angela flushed with annoyance. It was quite true that she looked down on Carlotta and always had – but she had hoped that Carlotta had not thought of it the last term or two. Carlotta had a very sharp tongue, and lashed out unmercifully at any one she disliked.

Hilary hurried on, hoping to avert a quarrel between the hot-tempered Carlotta and the annoyed Angela. "This is Angela," she said. "Our dream of beauty!"

"You've forgotten the Honourable," said a malicious voice – Carlotta's. "The *Honourable* Angela Favorleigh! Angela must have her label."

"Shut up, Carlotta," said Hilary. Angela scowled, making her lovely face quite ugly for a moment. Then she tossed her head and went out of the room. She had learnt by now that beauty and wealth were no match for a sharp wit like Carlotta's. Angela might be the most beautiful girl in the school and the richest, but Carlotta could always defeat her in a squabble.

"This is Pam, the brains of the form," said Hilary, pulling a plain, undergrown girl forward, with great big glasses

10

on her short-sighted eyes. "She works much too hard, but nobody can stop her!"

Some one peeped in at the door. It was Claudine, come to see if her aunt was still there.

"It's all right. Mam'zelle is still looking for you, but not here," said Carlotta. "Anne-Marie, this is Claudine, the Bad Girl of the form – she only works at what she likes, she always gets what she wants – and she doesn't care how she does it. She has been here quite a long time already, trying to learn what she calls 'the English sense of honour' – but she hasn't even smelt it yet!"

"Ah, you bad Carlotta," said the good-humoured Claudine. "Always you make fun of me. I am not so bad, and not so good."

Mirabel and Gladys were pulled forward, and the plain, quiet Pauline, who had once been as big a boaster as Angela, but had learnt a bitter lesson, and was now a much nicer girl.

"There you are – that's the lot," said Hilary, "except Felicity, our musical genius, who is coming up from the fourth form, and hasn't arrived yet – and Alma Pudden who comes down from the sixth. I haven't seen her about yet, either."

"I hope *you* don't do anything wonderful!" said Bobby, to Anne-Marie. "What with Pam's brilliant brains, and Angela's film-star beauty, and Felicity's musical genius, the fifth form has got enough wonderful people in it! I hope you're a nice ordinary person, Anne-Marie."

"Well – I'm not," said Anne-Marie, flushing red. "I'm – I'm a poet."

There was a deep silence after this. A poet! What exactly did Anne-Marie mean by that?

"What do you mean – you write poetry, or something?" said Bobby. "Oh, help!"

"You can't help being a poet, if you are one," said Anne-Marie. "You're born a poet. My grandfather was a famous poet, and my great-aunt was a great writer. It's in the family – and it's come out in me, I suppose. I'm always writing

11

poetry. Mostly in the middle of the night."

"Help!" said Bobby, again. "We've had many queer things at St. Clare's – but not a poet, as far as I remember. You and Felicity will make a pair! She gets up in the middle of the night to write a tune – you get up to write poems! Well – you'll be able to keep each other company!"

Another girl put her head in at the door and the twins yelled to her. "Alison! Where have you been? Come and be introduced to our poet."

A pretty, dainty girl came into the room, smiling. It was the twins' cousin, Alison.

"This is Alison," said Pat. "Our little featherhead. Thinks of nothing but her hair and her complexion an whether she has a shiny nose, and . . ."

Alison would have scowled, or burst into tears a few terms before, at this candid introduction, but she was thicker-skinned now. She merely lunged out at Pat, and nodded amiably at Anne-Marie.

"You'd better look out, Claudine," she said, "your aunt is coming along the passage."

"You can't escape now," said Hilary. "You've got to go through with it – go on, it pleases old Mam'zelle. She really is fond of you, goodness knows why!"

Mam'zelle swept into the room, saw Claudine and flung herself on her. "*Ma petite* Claudine! How are you? How are your dear father and mother, and all the family? I have seen the little Antoinette – ah, how lonely and shy the poor child looked. I have cakes and biscuits for you both in my room – you will come now, this very minute, and eat them with me!"

Claudine let herself be taken off. The others laughed. "Funny to think of Claudine being a fifth-former! Perhaps she will turn over a new leaf now she's so high up in the school."

But that was the last thing Claudine meant to do. She went her own way, saying what she pleased, doing what she pleased, and always would. It was surprising that so many people liked her!

12

Studies of Their Own

It was the rule at St. Clare's that as soon as any girl had been in the fifth form for two terms she should be allowed to have a small study of her own, which she shared with one other girl. These studies were tiny places, and the girls could, if they wished, furnish them themselves, though the school provided such things as a table, chairs and a carpet and shelves.

Most girls contented themselves with putting up a picture or so, and a clock. A few were more ambitious and got a carpet from home, and maybe even an armchair.

The girls themselves chose the companion with whom they wanted to share a study. This was not usually difficult, because by the time they reached the top forms the girls had all more or less made their own friends, and, when they were in the fourth form, had planned with whom they were going to share the study.

It was fun arranging about the studies. The pairs had to go to Matron and tell her they were going to share a study, and then Matron would allot one to them.

"Fancy *you* having a study!" she would say. "Dear me – it seems no time at all since you were in the first form and I nearly gave you a spanking for not reporting your sore throats to me!"

Pat and Isabel O'Sullivan were to share a study, of course. Mirabel and Gladys wanted to as well. Angela had asked Alison to share with her – both girls had the same dainty tastes.

"I bet there will be nothing but mirrors all the way round the walls of your study!" said Bobby to Alison. It was a standing joke that Alison always looked into any mirror she passed, or even in the glass of pictures, to see if her hair was all right.

13

Bobby and Janet were to share a study. Both were tomboys, with a love for practical jokes. What tricks would be
hatched out, in their study!

One odd pair was Pam Boardman, the brainy one of the
form, and Doris Edward, who was always near the bottom.
For all her brilliance at mimicry and acting, Doris could not
do ordinary lessons well, and admired Pam's brains deeply.
Pam had tried to help the bigger girl at times, and a warm
friendship had sprung up between them, which made Doris
suggest sharing a study. Pam had left St. Clare's once, but
had missed it so much that her parents had sent her back
again some time later.

The lonely little Pam, who had never had a real friend, at
once welcomed the idea of sharing a study with Doris. Doris
made her laugh, she teased her and put on her big glasses
and mimicked her. She was good for Pam.

"Whom is Carlotta going with?" wondered Pat. "Hilary,
perhaps. They like one another very much."

But no – Hilary, as head-girl of the form, had the honour
of a study all to herself. So Carlotta could not share with
her. She chose Claudine!

Matron was openly doubtful about this.

"You'll have a mighty bad effect on each other," she said.
"You're both as cheeky and don't-carish as can be. What
you'll be like if you share a study, I can't think. But mind –
any broken furniture or reports of rowdiness, and you'll go
down to the common room of the fourth formers."

"Oh, Matron – how can you think that we should be
rowdy?" said Claudine, putting on her most innocent look.
"I shall keep our study beautifully, so beautifully. Did I not
in the holidays embroider two table-cloths, and three cushion-covers for our study?"

Anne-Marie and Felicity were to share a study, although
Felicity had not been two terms in the fifth form, and Anne-
Marie was new. Matron did not want them to be the only
two without a study.

"Two geniuses together," said Bobby, with a laugh.

14

"They ought to use up the midnight oil all right, writing poems and tunes!"

No one had asked Pauline to share a study with them, and she had no friend to ask. She was not a girl that any one liked much, for she was envious, and had been very boastful till the others had found out that all her wonderful tales were made up. She had gone into her shell, and no one knew quite what the real Pauline was like.

"You had better share with Alma Pudden," said Matron, ticking them off on the list. "You're the only two left."

"Oh," said Pauline, dismally. She didn't like Alma very much. Nobody did. She was so fat and unwieldy and bad-tempered. But there was no one else to share with, so that was that.

"Well – that's the lot of you," said Matron, shutting her book. "You all know the study-rules, don't you? You can have your teas there by yourselves, if you don't want to go to the dining-room. You can get in some one from the first or second form to do any little job you want done. You can do your prep. there in the evenings, and you can go up to bed when you want to, providing it is not after ten o'clock."

The girls felt free and independent, having little rooms of their own. The studies were cosy corners, dens, bits of home – they could be arranged how the girls liked, and the tiny fire-places could burn cosy fires to sit by.

Angela, of course, furnished hers like a miniature palace. She bundled out every bit of the school furniture there, and got her mother to send her down things from her own bed-room. She went down to the town with Alison, and the two had a wonderful time choosing curtain material, cushion-covers and rugs.

They cost a lot of money. Alison hadn't very much, but Angela had had magnificent tips from wealthy uncles and aunts in the holidays, and had saved them up for her study. She spent lavishly, and would let no one into their room till it was finished.

Then she and Alison gave a "house-warming" as they

called it. They had ordered in cakes and sandwiches from the local baker, and bought lemonade and ginger-beer. The table was loaded with eatables, and a bright fire burnt in the grate, though the day was far too hot.

The girls crowded in curiously. They gasped at the polished furniture, beautiful mirrors and pictures, the two armchairs, and the lovely rugs. They fingered the silk curtains and looked at the brilliant chrysanthemums in the vases.

"Well!" said Bobby, "just wait till Matron sees all this! She'll tell Miss Theobald you have too much money to spend, Angela!"

"I don't see that it's anything to do with Matron," said Angela, stiffly. "Alison and I don't consider there is enough beauty or comfort at St. Clare's – not as much as *we* are used to at home, anyway – and now that we have a study of our own, we don't see why we can't fill it with our own ideas. Don't you like it, Bobby?"

"Well – it's a bit too showy for me," said Bobby. "You know my simple tastes! But you certainly have made a marvellous job of it, Angela – and this tea is super!"

The other girls added what they wanted to their studies. Claudine put out her embroidered table-cloths and cushion-covers. Carlotta added a few things she had brought from Spain, one thing especially giving the little study colour and character – a deep red embroidered shawl from Seville.

The only people whose study was quite plain and without character was the one shared by Pauline and Alma. Neither of them had any taste or much money, and except for a blue vase contributed by Pauline and a tea-cosy as plump as Alma herself given by Alma, the little study was as bare as in the holidays.

Alma Pudden had a most unfortunate name. It would not have mattered a bit if she hadn't been so like a suet pudding to look at, but she was. Her school tunic always looked like a sack tied round in the middle. Her eyes were almost hidden in her round, pasty face.

It was the fifth formers who nicknamed her Pudding, and

she hated it, which was not to be wondered at. If she had laughed, and said "Yes, I *am* rather puddingy – but I shall thin out soon!" the others would probably have liked her, and called her Pudding more in affection than in derision. But Alma flew into one of her bad rages when she was teased.

She had queer tempers – not hot ones, quickly flaring up and down, like Carlotta's or Janet's – but cold, spiteful rages. Try as they would the others could not like anything about poor Alma.

Poor Pauline found sharing a study with Alma very dull indeed. Alma seldom had any intelligent remark to make, and though she pored over her prep. she rarely got good marks. She was selfish too, and always took the more comfortable chair, and helped herself to more cakes than Pauline.

Felicity and Anne-Marie found it rather trying to live together in the same study. Felicity thought there was nothing in the world but music, and she was always singing or trying out tunes on her violin, when Anne-Marie wanted to work or to write.

"Felicity! *Must* you play that awful, gloomy tune again?" Anne-Marie would say. "I'm trying to get the last verse of this poem right."

"What poem? Is it the one you were doing last week?" Felicity would say. "Well, it's a dreadful poem – all words and no meaning. You are no poet, Anne-Marie. Why should I stop my music in order that you should write third-rate poetry?"

Felicity did not mean to be rude or even hurtful. She was, as Bobby said, quite "batty" about her music. She was working for a stiff exam., the L.R.A.M. and was very young indeed to take it. Miss Theobald, the Head Mistress, did not want her to work for it, and had already told Felicity's people that the girl must live an ordinary life, and take more interest in ordinary things.

"She is growing one-sided," Miss Theobald explained to

Felicity's parents, who came to see her one day. "Sometimes I think she doesn't live in this world at all! That is bad for a young girl. She is already far too old for the fourth form, and yet is not fit to do the work of the fifth. But I think I had better put her up into the fifth, where the girls there of her own age will wake her up a bit. I wish you would say that Felicity must put off working for this difficult music exam. for a year or two. She has plenty of time before her!"

But Felicity's people were too proud of their brilliant daughter to put off any exam. It would be wonderful to have a girl who was the youngest to pass such an exam.!

"Put her up in the fifth form if you wish, Miss Theobald," said Felicity's father. "But don't let her slacken in any way in her music studies. We have been told she is a genius, and a genius must be helped and encouraged in every way."

"Of course," said the Head Mistress, "but we must be sure that our ways of encouragement are the *right* ones, surely. I don't like all this hard, musical work for so young a girl, when it means that other, quite necessary work has to be scamped."

But it was no use talking like that to Felicity's parents. Their girl was brilliant, and she must go on being even more brilliant! And so it was that Felicity was put up into the fifth form, to be with girls of her own age even though her work was far below the form's standard – and yet had to work even harder at her music than before.

She did not like or dislike Anne-Marie. She was there and had to be put up with, but so long as she did not interfere too much with her music, Felicity did not really notice her study companion.

But Anne-Marie was jealous of Felicity and her undoubted genius. Anne-Marie was convinced that she too was a genius. Her people were sure she was, as well. They had her best poems framed, they recited them to visitors, who were too polite to say what they really thought, and tried to get publishers to print them.

It was most annoying that the girls at St. Clare's didn't

18

seem to think anything of her loveliest poems. There was that one beginning:

> Down the long lanes of the Future
> My tear-bedimmed eyes are peering,

Only Angela and Alma had been impressed with it. Neither of them had enough brains to know a good poem from a bad one, and they could not see the would-be cleverness and insincerity of the long and ostentatious poem.

"What's it *mean*?" said Carlotta. "I may be very stupid, but I don't understand a word of it. Why are your eyes tear-bedimmed, Anne-Marie? Are you so afraid of your future? Well, I'm not surprised, if that's the way you're going to earn your living! You won't get much money."

"It's tosh," said Bobby. "You write something you really *feel*, Anne-Marie, and maybe you'll get something good out of your mind. This is all pretence – just trying to be awfully grown-up when you're not."

So Anne-Marie was bitterly disappointed that *her* genius was not recognized, whilst every one apparently agreed that Felicity was gifted.

Still, on the whole, the study companions got on fairly well, some of them much better than others, of course. The twins rarely quarrelled, and had so much of the same tastes and likings that sharing a study was, for them, a thing of delight. Bobby and Janet too were very happy together, and so were Mirabel and Gladys.

It was queer at first to get used to sending for the younger ones to do odd jobs. But on the whole that was quite a good idea too. Many of the first formers, for instance, had been head-girls, or at least in the top forms of their prep. schools, and it did them good to be at the bottom of another school, having, at times, to rush off to do the bidding of the older girls. The twins remembered how they had hated it at first.

"We thought it was beneath our dignity to light someone's fire, do you remember?" said Pat to Isabel, as she poked up the fire that a first former had just been in to light for her. "It was jolly good for us. We were so stuck up – thought such a lot of ourselves too! We got our corners rubbed off all right."

"We get to know the younger ones too," said Isabel. "They chatter away to us when they come to do their jobs. I'm getting to like some of the little first formers very much. One or two of them will be very good at games – they are awfully keen."

"Angela sends for the young ones far too much, though," said Pat, frowning. "She and Alison make them do too many jobs. They've got a bit of power, and they are using it badly."

"Better get Hilary to tick them off," said Isobel, yawning. "Golly, it's five to ten. Come on, we'd better pack up and go to bed. Isn't it fun to go when we like?"

"So long as it's not after ten o'clock!" said Pat imitating Matron's crisp voice. "Hurry – or it *will* be after ten!"

The New English Teacher

That term there were a great many more girls at St. Clare's in the younger forms, and Miss Theobald decided to engage an extra mistress, to take some of the work off the shoulders of the class-mistresses.

So, to the interest of all the girls, Miss Willcox appeared. She was present at Assembly the second day and looked round with vague, rather soulful eyes.

"Her name's Miss Willcox," the girls whispered to one another. "She's awfully clever. She's going to take English. She writes! She has had a book of poetry published."

The girls all gazed at Miss Willcox with awe. They thought that any one must indeed be clever to have written a book. Miss Willcox gazed back at the girls, her eyes dreamy and far away. What could she be thinking of? Another book, perhaps?

It was always exciting to have a new teacher. What would

she be like in class? Strict? Humorous? Lenient? Dull? Would she be a good one to play a few tricks on?

"I think she looks most interesting," said Alison. "I do really. I think she looks as if all kinds of beautiful thoughts are passing through her mind."

"She's probably wondering what there will be for lunch," said Bobby. "I always suspect those people that look dreamily into the distance. Anne-Marie does it sometimes, and I know jolly well that half the time she's wondering if Felicity has remembered to get the cakes for tea, or something like that, and the other half she's thinking of nothing at all."

Anne-Marie wished she could think of something smart to say back, but she never could. Well – poets were always misunderstood, she knew that. People laughed at them, and jeered at their work – but then, years after they were dead, people said how wonderful they were.

"Perhaps Miss Willcox will know that I am a real poet," she thought. "It would be nice to have some one on my side. I daresay if Miss Willcox reads my poems and likes them she will make the others change their minds. I'll work awfully hard in her classes, and get on her good side."

Miss Willcox's lessons were certainly interesting. They were filled with plays and poetry, and the girls were allowed to debate anything they liked, so long as it had to do with literature.

There was no doubt that Miss Willcox "knew her stuff" as Bobby put it. She was very widely read, had an excellent memory, and really did know how to pick out things that would interest the girls, and make them think.

She was a strange woman to look at, though – untidy, vague and given to "bits and pieces" as Janet said. A scarf wound round her neck, a brilliant belt, a very striking handkerchief. She wore gold-headed pins in her black hair, and her dresses all had a drapy look about them. They did not really fit her.

She had an affected voice which rather spoilt her reading of poetry, for she pitched it deep and low, when really it

21

should have been quite ordinary. She had graceful, dramatic gestures, which filled Alison's romantic soul with delight.

Alison copied one or two of the gestures. She flung out her hand dramatically when she was telling Pat and Isabel something, and hit Bobby with the back of her fingers.

"Hey!" said Bobby. "Our feather-head is copying Miss Willcox! Alison, you're not going to lose your heart to *her*, are you?"

Alison went red. She always blushed very easily, which annoyed her. "I don't know what you mean," she said. "I admire Miss Willcox, I must say. Her knowledge of English literature is marvellous."

"Oh, Alison!" groaned Bobby. "Don't say you're going to worship Miss Willcox. Haven't you got over that silly habit yet? You never choose the right people to worship, either!"

"Why isn't Miss Willcox the right person?" said Alison trying to speak coldly, though she felt very hot and cross. "She's clever – she's written a book of most marvellous poetry – she's got a lovely deep voice, and I think she's most picturesque-looking."

"Untidy and messy, you mean," said Bobby, in disgust. "Picturesque-looking, indeed! What an idiot you are, Alison. I think Miss Willcox wants smartening up and making tidy. Gold-topped pins in her hair – gosh, it nearly made me sick to see them."

Bobby was going to extremes and did not mean all she said. She was such a downright, boyish person, she so much hated nonsense and show, that people like Miss Willcox made her "go off the deep end" and say more than she meant.

"Oh, Miss Willcox is not so bad as you make out, Bobby," said Pat, seeing that Alison looked as if she was about to burst into tears. "And she's not so wonderful as *you* make out, either, Alison. Anyway – for goodness' sake don't put on a worshipping act this term. You've been fairly sensible the last two terms or so."

Alison turned away. "Remember Miss Quentin," said

Bobby, warningly. "Don't make the same mistake again!"

Miss Quentin had been worshipped by Alison when she was in a lower form, and Alison had been bitterly hurt by her, because she had found out that the mistress was laughing at her behind her back. She had learnt a hard lesson then and had been more careful whom she gave her heart to. But now it looked as if she was going to start all over again!

"It's no good trying to stop her," said Pat, watching her cousin as she left the room, her head high in the air, and her cheeks burning. "You only make her worse, Bobby. She goes all loyal and intense."

"Well, I've said my say," said Bobby. "It wouldn't matter a bit if only Alison would choose somebody decent, but she never does."

"If Miss Willcox was sensible she'd nip Alison in the bud," said Pat. "Miss Cornwallis soon nips any silliness in the bud! So do the other mistresses. I can see that Miss Willcox is going to encourage that awful Anne-Marie too."

"Well – let her!" said Bobby. "If she wants the Alisons and Anne-Maries of the world sitting at her feet, she's welcome to them. Come on – let's go and see if the court is hard enough for tennis."

They passed Alma Pudden on the way out. The girl looked rather dull and miserable. Pat felt sorry for her.

"Come and have a game!" she called. "Make up a four."

"I can't run," said Alma, in her usual dull voice. "I'm too fat."

"Well, it will get your fat down a bit," said Isabel. "Come on!"

But no – Alma was almost as obstinate at refusing any exercise as Claudine was. Claudine got out of all games if she could, and even out of the nature walks. At first she had arranged matters so that Matron piled mending on her, which had to be done in games times – but Matron had got wise to this little trick after a time, and Claudine suddenly found that she had not enough mending to make an excuse for missing out-door life.

23

But Claudine was not to be defeated in anything. If she did have to put on games clothes and shoes, and appear on the field or court, she would be taken with violent cramps, or would feel sick, and have to go off. It was simply amazing how she managed to slide out of the things she disliked.

She and Carlotta were a real pair in their study. Carlotta would not do things she disliked either, if she could get out of them but she used open and direct methods, whereas Claudine really enjoyed getting her way secretly, putting on an innocent face all the time.

They both made war against Mirabel, who, to her intense delight, had been made sports captain for the school that term, as she had hoped. Gladys had been made vice-captain, and this pleased them both. Gladys was small, but very quick and deft on the playing-field or tennis court, and a fine little swimmer. Also, she was very good at dealing with some of the shy, younger girls, who were a bit afraid of Mirabel's heartiness and drive.

Mirabel was a typical sports captain, loud-voiced, hearty in manner, strapping in figure, and not very sensitive to the feelings of others. She was always trying to make Alison, Claudine, Angela and Carlotta take more interest in the games, and they were just as determined not to. It annoyed her intensely when they would not turn up at practices she had arranged, or got bored on the field and talked.

"This Mirabel, she is a pest," complained Claudine to her aunt, Mam'zelle. "Always she wants me to go to the field and make myself hot and dirty and untidy. Can you not tell her my heart is weak, *ma tante*?"

"Claudine! Have you a weak heart, my child? This you have never told me before!" cried Mam'zelle, in alarm. "Have you a pain? You must go to Matron."

This was the last thing that Claudine wanted to do. Matron was the one person who constantly disbelieved all that Claudine said.

"No, I have no pain," said Claudine, demurely. "Only just a little flutter here – and now and again when I run or

24

go up the stairs."

Mam'zelle looked at Claudine hard. She loved her dearly, but it did sometimes cross her mind that her niece might deceive her in order to gain her own ends. Claudine had pressed her hand over the place where she thought her heart was, to show where the fluttter came – but unfortunately she wasn't indicating the right place.

"*Tiens!*" said Mam'zelle, half-alarmed still but a little angry. "That is not your heart. That is your stomach. Maybe you need a dose of good medicine."

Claudine disappeared at once. She was not going to have any of Matron's good medicine. She made up her mind to find out exactly where her heart was, so that another time she would not make a mistake.

After a few days the fifth form settled down into their usual familiar routine. They tackled their new work, grumbled and groused, laughed and talked, played games and went to bed tired out. It was a good life, an interesting, full and friendly one. Sometimes the fifth formers felt a little sad when they thought that they had only one more form to go into – and then St. Clare's would be left behind for ever.

There was to be a stiff exam. half-way through the term, which every one was to take, even Doris and Alma and Felicity, who felt absolutely certain they would not be able to pass it.

"But it won't do you any harm to work for it," said Miss Cornwallis, in her crisp voice. "If you could just get a Pass I should feel you had achieved something! I shall allow you to relax, all of you, after the exam. is over, but I must insist that you do your very best for the first half of the term, and really study hard."

So there was some very hard work done in the little studies that term. Carlotta groaned over her maths and Claudine puzzled over grammar. Felicity tried to learn her English literature and to write essays which usually ended abruptly because she had suddenly thought of a new tune. Anne-Marie rushed through all her prep. except the English and

25

then spent laborious hours over that, hoping to win approval from Miss Willcox.

Even Doris and Angela worked, though neither of them liked it. School was fun – but it *was* hard work too!

Angela Loses Her Temper

The little first formers came and went at the bidding of the fifth. They ran errands, they made toast for tea and they chattered about their affairs to any one who would listen.

Mirabel was always kindest to those who were good at games. She encouraged them to practise well at catching and running for lacrosse, she made up the teams for the school, and coached them well in her spare time. The younger girls thought she was wonderful.

"You know, that little Molly Williams is awfully good," said Mirabel to Gladys, when she was making up the teams one day. "I've a good mind to let her play in the third team, Gladys. And Jane Teal is good too, if she would practise running a bit more. She could be quite fast."

"Little Antoinette is just as bad as Claudine," said Gladys. "I can't get her to practise at all, or to take any interest in games. Claudine doesn't back us up there, either. She is always telling Antoinette good excuses to make."

"I'm tired of Claudine and her silly ways," said Mirabel, impatiently. "She's cunning. She'll get herself expelled one day!"

"Oh, no – she isn't as bad as that," said Gladys, quite shocked. "She's just different from us that's all. She's better than she was."

"I should hope so, after all these terms at St. Clare's," said Mirabel, writing the list of girls for the third team. "Well – I've put Molly Williams down – she'll be thrilled."

"It's a pity Angela and Alison order the young ones about

26

so much," said Gladys. "They have always got one or other of them in their study, doing something for them. Angela even got Jane Teal in to do some mending for her, and that's not allowed."

"I'll speak to Jane about it," said Mirabel, in her direct way. "I'll tell her she's not supposed to do Angela's mending, and she must use that time to get out on the practice field."

"Well – wouldn't it be better to tell Angela that, not Jane?" said Gladys. "It would come better from Angela, if she told Jane to stop doing her mending, than it would from you."

"I'll deal with Jane myself," said Mirabel, very much the sports captain, rather over-bearing and arrogant that morning.

"Jane's fond of Angela," said Gladys, as Mirabel went out of the room. Mirabel snorted.

"She looks up to *me* no end," she said. "I'm pretty certain she'll do what *I* want, and not what Angela says. You really can leave these things to me, Gladys."

Mirabel found Jane Teal and called to her. "Hie Jane! Come here a minute!"

The fourteen-year-old Jane, small, slight and quick, went to Mirabel, her face flushing. She wondered if Mirabel was going to tell her she was to play in the third team with Molly. What a thrill that would be!

"Jane," said Mirabel, in her direct way, "I want you to do a bit more practising in the field the next few weeks. You'll be good if you really do practise. You ought to have been out this week. I hear you've been doing Angela's mending instead, and you know you don't need to do that."

"I like to," said Jane, flushing again. "I'm good at sewing and Angela isn't. I like doing things for her."

"Well, you give that up and pay more attention to games," said Mirabel. "I'm in charge of games and I want the good players doing their best."

"I will do my best," said Jane, proud to hear the great Mirabel say that she was one of the good players. "But I did promise Angela to do all her mending this term – at least I offered to, Mirabel."

"Well, you must tell her you can't," said Mirabel, who quite failed to see that anything mattered except what she wanted herself.

"But – she'll be very cross and upset – and I do like doing things for her," said Jane, half-frightened, but obstinate. "I – I think she's beautiful, Mirabel. Don't you?"

"I don't see what that's got to do with it," said Mirabel, impatiently. "Anyway, I'm your sports captain and you've got to do as you're told. If you don't, I shan't let you play in even the fourth team, let alone the third."

Mirabel's tone was sharp. She turned on her heel and went off. Jane looked after her, and tears smarted in her eyes. She admired Mirabel so much – and she did like Angela so much too. Angela had such a lovely smile and she said such nice things. The other girl she shared her study with was nice too – Alison.

Jane went to find her friend, Sally. She told her all that Mirabel had said and Sally listened.

"Well," said Sally, "you'll have to do what Mirabel tells you if you want to play in the third team and have some good matches. Why don't you go to Angela and tell her what Mirabel has said? You know quite well that if she is as sweet and kind as you say she is, she'll say at once that of course you mustn't do her mending any more."

"Oh – that's a good idea," said Jane, looking happier. "I couldn't bear to upset Angela, Sally. I do really think she's wonderful. I should be miserable if she was angry with me."

"Tell her when you go and make toast for her tea today," said Sally. So that afternoon, rather tremblingly, Jane began to tell Angela what Mirabel had said.

"Angela," she began, putting a piece of bread on to the toasting-fork, "Angela, I've brought your mending back. I've done everything, even that stocking that had a ladder all the way down the back of the leg."

28

"Thanks, Jane," said Angela and gave Jane a smile that thrilled her.

"But – I don't believe I'll be able to do it much more," went on Jane.

"Why ever not?" demanded Angela. "You promised you would. I hate people who back out of things when they have promised to do them."

"Well, you see – Mirabel spoke to me about it today," said Jane, rather desperately. "She said – she said –"

"Oh, I can guess what she said," said Angela sneeringly. "She said you were a wonderful player – and you must practise more – and you mustn't do odd jobs for that horrid Angela. And you meekly said you wouldn't. Little turn-coat."

"Oh Angela, don't talk like that," said poor Jane. "It's not fair. Of course Mirabel didn't speak against you. But I have to do what she says, don't I? She's sports captain."

"I don't see why *any* one has to do what dear, hearty, loud-voiced Mirabel says!" said Angela. "I don't see why because *she's* mad on something she should expect every one else to be mad on it too. This passion for games, games, games! I agree with Claudine that it's silly."

"Oh but Angela," said Jane, shocked, "games are lovely. And they make you get the team-spirit too, and play for your side instead of yourself – and –"

"Don't preach at *me*," said Angela, angrily. "You're only a half-baked first former. I don't care what you do, anyway. Go and practise running and catching morning, noon, and night if you want to. I shall certainly not allow you to do anything for me in future. I don't like turn-coats. Leave that toast and go and find Violet Hill and send her to me. She can do my jobs instead of you."

Jane was horrified at this outburst. She had given her heart to the beautiful, radiant Angela, and now it was treated as rubbish! Angela didn't want her any more. She would have that silly Violet Hill, who adored Angela from afar and would do anything for a smile from her.

Jane gave a sob and rushed out of theroom. In a few minutes Violet Hill came in, thrilled to be sent for. Angela gave her orders in a lazy voice, amused to see how the little first former almost trembled with excitement as she tidied up the room, and hung on Angela's lightest word.

Alison came in after a while and looked surprised to see Violet there instead of Jane. "Where's our devoted Jane?" she asked.

Angela told her in a few words what had happened. Violet Hill listened eagerly. She was glad that Jane was in disgrace. She would show Angela how much nicer she, Violet, was!

When Violet went out Alison spoke rather shortly to Angela. "You shouldn't have said all that in front of Violet. You know how keen Jane was on you – she'll have a fit if she knows all this will be passed round her form."

"Serves her right," said Angela, viciously.

"Angela, you make these kids awfully silly," said Alison, after a pause. "I don't really think you treat them properly. You oughtn't to let them think you're so wonderful. I bet poor Jane is crying her eyes out. You know Miss Theobald dislikes that kind of thing."

Angela went pale with rage. She always hated being found fault with. She glared at Alison and tried to think of something really cutting. She found what she wanted at last.

"Really, Alison," she said, in her lightest, most jeering voice, "really, Alison – who are *you* to talk of thinking people wonderful! You're a perfect ninny over that wonderful Miss Willcox of yours, aren't you? Why, you're even trying to copy that deep voice of hers. It just makes me laugh."

Alison was deeply hurt. When she was fond of any one she could not bear to hear a single word said against them.

"Miss Willcox is an absolutely sincere person," she said, with dignity. "That's why I like her. You've no interest in English literature, or anything at all really, except yourself, Angela – so you can't understand my admiring any one with such an interesting character as Miss Willcox."

"Tosh," said Angela, rudely.

The two girls said no more to each other that evening. Angela fumed in silence and Alison wrote a long and, as she fondly hoped, intelligent essay for Miss Willcox. It was not a very happy evening.

Angela had her knife into Mirabel after that. She did not dare to go and tackle Mirabel openly about Jane, because she was afraid of Mirabel's rudeness. Mirabel was tasting power for the first time as sports captain, and she was rather arrogant and blunt in her speech. Also she was very thick-skinned and Angela despaired of being able to say anything that would hurt her.

So she had to content herself with looking at her sneer-ingly, and saying mocking things behind her back. But as sneering glances and words were typical of Angela when she was upset about something, no one took much notice, Mira-bel least of all.

Angela made things up with Alison, not so much because she wanted to, but because she simply had to have some one to talk to and air her views to. Also, Alison genuinely ad-mired her looks and her clothes, and it was always pleasant to bask in admiration of that sort.

Alison was not foolish with Angela as she had been when she first came. She no longer spoilt her and praised her and agreed with everything. But she could not hide her real admiration of the lovely girl with her shining golden hair, and brilliant blue eyes.

She was glad to make up the quarrel with Angela, for she wanted to talk about Miss Willcox – how wonderful she was in class, what beautiful poetry she wrote, how well she re-cited in that soulful voice of hers.

So, in return for admiration, Angela listened, rather bored, to all that Alison wanted to say. They were friends again – but it would not take much to turn them into enemies once more!

31

Hard Work – and a Little Fun

The fifth form were certainly working hard. Miss Cornwallis kept their noses to the grindstone, as Pat said, and piled prep. on to them. Miss Willcox expected a great deal of them too. Miss Theobald, the Head, took the form for one or two lessons and although she did not give them a great deal of prep. the girls felt that what she did give them must be specially well done.

When Mam'zelle piled prep. on them too, the girls grew indignant. "Gracious! What with all that maths. to do, and that map to draw, and those French poems to memorize, and that essay for Miss Willcox, we'll all have nervous break-downs!" groaned Bobby.

Only Pam Boardman did not seem to mind. She had an amazing memory, and had only to look at a page once to know it by heart. Doris envied her this gift from the bottom of her heart.

"I've no memory at all for lessons," she sighed. "What I learn in the morning I've forgotten in the evening."

"Well, if you're going to be an actress, you'll have parts to learn, won't you?" said Pam.

"The funny thing is, when I act a part and say the words out loud, I can remember them quite easily," said Doris. "I never forget them then. It's sitting hunched up over a book, reading and re-reading the words that gets me down."

"Well, Doris, stand up and recite the words out loud, and act them if you want to," said Pam, a gleam of fun coming into her solemn eyes. "Here – take this French poem – it's all about the so-beautiful country-side, as Mam'zelle would say. Recite it out loud, act the cows and the sheep, frisk when you come to the part where the little lambs play, and waddle like a duck when you get to them. You'll soon learn it."

Doris declaimed the poem loudly

So, to the amazement of Pat and Isabel, who looked in at Pam's study to borrow a book, Doris threw herself heart, soul and body into the French pastoral poem.

She declaimed the poem loudly, with gestures of all kinds. She frisked like a lamb, she chewed cud like a cow, she waddled like a duck. It was perfect.

The girls shrieked with laughter. Doris had turned the solemn and rather heavy French poem into a real comedy.

"Now – do you know it?" said Pam, when Doris finished, and sat down panting in a chair.

Doris screwed up her nose and thought hard. "Let me see," she said, "it begins like this . . ."

But until she got up and acted the poem as she had done before, she could not remember a word. It was evidently the acting that brought the words to her mind.

"Well – you do know the poem," said Pam, pleased. "You won't forget it now. Mam'zelle will be pleased with her *chère* Doris tomorrow!"

Doris, however, was not in Mam'zelle's good books the next day. Her French exercise was nothing but mistakes and was slashed right across with Mam'zelle's thick blue pencil. Mam'zelle never spared her blue pencil when she was annoyed, and a page disapproved of by her was always a terrible sight.

"Ah, you Doris!" began Mam'zelle, when she was going through the work with her class. "You! Have I had you on my thumb . . ."

"Under my thumb," said Bobby, with a grin. Mam'zelle glared at her and resumed.

"Have I had you on my thumb for all these terms and still you do not know that a table is she not he. Why are you not in the kindergarten? Why can you still not pronounce the French R? All the others can. You are a great big stupid girl."

"Yes, Mam'zelle," said poor Doris, meekly. When Mam'zelle flew into a rage, it was best to be meek. But for some reason Doris's meekness irritated Mam'zelle even more.

"Ah – you mock at me now! 'Yes, Mam'zelle' you

34

say, with your tongue in your mouth and butter melting in your cheek!" cried Mam'zelle, getting things mixed up as usual.

The girls giggled. "You mean, with your tongue in your cheek, and butter that won't melt in your mouth," suggested Bobby again.

"Do not tell me what I mean, Bobbee," said Mam'zelle, exasperated. "Always you interrupt. Doris, stand up."

Doris stood up, her humorous mouth twitching. She would act this scene afterwards for the benefit of the girls. How they would laugh!

"Your written work is very bad. Now let me hear your oral work," demanded Mam'zelle. "You have learnt the French poem? Yes – then let me hear it. Begin!"

Doris couldn't think of a single word. She stared into the distance, racking her brains. She knew there were all kinds of animals in it – but how did the words go?

"She did learn it, Mam'zelle," said Pam's voice, earnestly. "I heard her say it all through without looking at the book once."

"Then I too will hear it now," said Mam'zelle. "Begin, Doris."

Pam sat just behind Doris. She whispered the first line to her. Doris began – and then she suddenly knew that if only she could act the poem, she could say every word – but not one line would come unless she acted it! Oh dear – she couldn't possibly act it in front of Mam'zelle, who loved French poetry, and would think she was making fun of it.

"Well, Doris, I wait. I wait patiently," said Mam'zelle, who was anything but patient at that moment. "Can you or can you not say the poem to me?"

"Yes. I can," said Doris. "But – but only if I act it."

"Then act it," said Mam'zelle, losing the last of her patience. "But if you are not telling me the truth, *ma chère* Doris, I complain to Miss Theobald. Act it – but say the poem through without a mistake."

So, in despair, Doris acted the French poem in her usual exaggerated, ridiculous manner, waggling herself, chewing

35

the cud, waddling, frisking – and, of course, as soon as she acted the poem, she knew it all the way through without a single mistake. She certainly had a queer memory.

The girls were thrilled and amused at Doris's rendering of the solemn poem, but they felt certain that Mam'zelle would be exceedingly angry. It was Claudine that saved the situation.

She clapped her hands in delight. She threw back her head and laughed her infectious laugh. She held her sides and almost doubled herself up.

"Oh *ma tante, ma tante!*" she cried to her aunt. "The clever Doris, the marvellous Doris! Such a poem she makes of it – and not one single mistake. Ah, never never shall I forget this poem now!"

Mam'zelle pushed her glasses on to her nose more firmly. Her face changed. She let out a roar of delighted laughter, and the class breathed loudly in relief. So long as Mam'zelle saw the joke it was all right.

Mam'zelle took off her glasses and wiped her streaming eyes. "It is clever, very clever, Doris," she said. "It is not the right way to recite such a poem, no. But it is very clever and very amusing. I will forgive you this time for your bad work. It is true that you know the poem, and you have made it very funny. Is it not so, Claudine?"

Claudine agreed. "We too will say the poem like that," she suggested, her eyes gleaming with fun. But Mam'zelle was not going so far as that.

"*Ah non!*" she said. "Doris has a gift that way. One girl is funny, but fourteen, fifteen girls would not be funny. *Tiens!* Look at the clock. We have wasted half the lesson on this bad, clever Doris. Get out your books, please."

Doris found that she could learn anything if only she said it out loud and put ridiculous actions to the words. But so often she could not repeat what she had learnt unless she accompanied it with absurd actions. Miss Willcox did not think this was funny. She called it "playing the fool" and said it was very bad taste.

As for doing such a thing in Miss Cornwallis's class or

Miss Theobald's, it was quite unthinkable. However much the girls begged Doris to recite the latest maths. rules with appropriate – or inappropriate – actions she would not.

"I'm not going to get expelled just to make you laugh," she said. "I must go on plodding away, and get Pam's help as much as I can. I'll never be any good at lessons."

"But you'll always be able to make people laugh!" said Isabel. "I'd almost rather do that than anything, but I'm not much good at it."

"I'd rather write a book or paint a beautiful picture," said Alison.

"So would I," said Anne-Marie. "Much rather. To leave something of oneself behind, something one has made or created – now that's really worth-while."

"Deirdre fans!" said Carlotta, mockingly.

Alison had found out that Miss Willcox's first initial was D. and had asked her what it stood for.

"Deirdre," said Miss Willcox, and Alison had thought it a most beautiful name, almost picturesque enough for her darling Miss Wilcox. Deirdre Willcox –a lovely name for a poet!

She had told Angela and Angela had told every one else. Both Anne-Marie and Alison were always round Miss Willcox, and the girls now called them "Deirdre fans". It annoyed them very much. Allison was sorry now that she had told any one Miss Willcox's name – she would have liked to be the only one that knew it.

She and Anne-Marie both vied with each other for Miss Willcox's attentions. Alison was jealous of Anne-Marie because she could write poetry, and Miss Willcox encouraged her to bring her her poems. Anne-Marie was jealous of Alison because she felt sure that Miss Willcox liked Alison the better of the two, which was quite true. A little of Anne-Marie and her intenseness went a very long way.

"You're both silly," said Bobby, who never could understand what she called "sloppiness". "Can't you see that any one who encourages a couple of idiots like you can't be worth sucking up to?"

37

But this kind of remark only made Alison and Anne-Marie more devoted. It even brought them together a little in their common indignation, which amused the girls very much. The "Deirdre fans" were the cause of a lot of fun that half-term!

Angela and the Younger Girls

Little Jane Teal turned up on the lacrosse field and practised zealously, much to Mirabel's satisfaction.

"There you are," she said to Gladys, triumphantly. "You see, a little plain talking has done Jane Teal a lot of good. I shall make her a very good player in no time."

Gladys had noticed that Jane had done exactly what Mirabel had told her, but she had also noticed too that Jane looked rather miserable.

"She doesn't seem very happy about it," she said. "And it doesn't seem to me that she puts much heart into all her practising. I bet Angela made things very unpleasant for her when she told her she couldn't do her mending any more."

"Oh, well – it's a good thing if Jane gets that sort of non-sense knocked out of her," said Mirabel. "I can't bear these kids that go round worshipping people."

"Well, a lot of them think no end of *you*," said Gladys, "and you like them to."

"That's different," said Mirabel at once. "They look up to me because I'm sports captain, because I make them work hard, and because I don't stand any nonsense. I should tick them off if they got sloppy over me."

"Well – all the same I think little Jane looks miserable," said Gladys. "Don't frown like that at me, Mirabel. After all, I'm your vice-captain, and I have a right to say what I think to you."

Mirabel looked in surprise at Gladys, who was often called

the Mouse, because she said so little and was so quiet. Mirabel was fond of Gladys – in fact she was the only girl in the school that she had any real affection for at all. All the same, she didn't think she could allow Gladys to find fault with her decisions – what was the sense of being captain if you didn't make your own decisions and stick to them? A little power had gone to Mirabel's head!

"You can say what you like to me, of course," said Mirabel, stiffly, "but that doesn't mean I shall pay attention to your suggestions, I'm afraid, Gladys. I shall *listen* to them, of course – but I am the one to decide everything."

Gladys said no more. Mirabel was not going to be a very easy person to live with that term! Gladys wished she was bold like Carlotta, or downright like Bobby, or a strong character like Hilary – they always seemed able to cope with others in the right way, but Gladys was afraid of hurting them, or of making them angry.

Angela made a fuss of Violet Hill, in order to punish poor Jane. She gave her one of her best hair-slides and a book, which sent the foolish Violet into transports of delight. Violet showed them to Jane and Sally.

"Look," she said, "isn't Angela a dear? She's so generous. I think she's wonderful. I do think you were silly to quarrel with her, Jane. I think Angela is worth three of Mirabel!"

Jane looked miserably at the book and the hair-slide. Angela had never given *her* a present. She wished she could dislike Angela, but she couldn't. Every time she saw the golden-haired girl, with her starry eyes set in her oval face, she thought how wonderful she was.

Sally was sorry for Jane. "Cheer up," she said. "Angela isn't worth worrying about. I believe she's only making up to Violet just to make you jealous. I think she's being beastly."

But Jane would not hear a word against Angela, however much she had been hurt by her. Violet too was cross at Sally's remarks.

"As if Angela would give me presents just to make Jane

jealous!'" she said, sharply. "If you ask *me*, I think she gave me them because I mended her blue jumper so neatly. It took me hours."

"Do you do her mending then?" said Jane, jealously.

"Of course," said Violet. "I don't care what Mirabel says to *me* – if I prefer to do things for Angela, I shall do them."

Violet told Angela how upset Jane was, and Angela was glad. She could be very spiteful when anything upset her. She was especially sweet to Violet and to the other first former who came when Violet could not come. The two of them thought she was the nicest girl in the whole school.

Antoinette, Claudine's sister, also at times had to do jobs for the fifth and sixth formers. She did not like Angela, and always found excuses not to go to her study, even when an urgent message was sent.

"That young sister of yours is a perfect nuisance," Angela complained to Claudine. "Can't you knock some sense into her, Claudine? When I sent for her yesterday, she sent back to say that she was doing her practising – and now I hear that she doesn't even *learn* music!"

"She might have been practising something else," suggested Claudine, politely. "Maybe lacrosse."

Angela snorted. "Don't be silly! Antoinette gets out of games just like you do – the very idea of thinking she might put in a bit of practice is absurd. I believe you encourage her in these bad ways – slipping out of anything she doesn't like."

Claudine looked shocked. "Ah, but surely the little Antoinette loves everything at this so-English school?"

"Don't pretend to me," said Angela, exasperated. "I should have thought that in all the terms you have been here, Claudine, you would have got more English – you're just as French as ever you were!"

Claudine would not lose her temper at this ungracious speech. "It is good to be French," she said, in her light, amiable voice. "If I were English I might have been *you*, Angela – and that I could not have borne. Better a hundred times to be a French Claudine than an English Angela!"

Angela could not think of any really good retort to this, and by the time she had found her tongue Claudine had gone over to speak to Mam'zelle. Angela knew she had gone to Mam'zelle on purpose – no one would dare to attack Claudine with Mam'zelle standing by! Mam'zelle was intensely loyal to her two nieces.

"All right," thought Angela, spitefully. "I'll just get that slippery sister of hers and make her do all kinds of things for me! I'll speak to Hilary about it, and she'll tell Antoinette she's jolly well got to come when I or Alison send for her."

Hilary knew that Antoinette was being very naughty about coming when she was sent for – but she knew too that Angela used the younger girls far too much. She used her prettiness and charm to make them into little slaves. So she was not very helpful to Angela when the girl told her about Antoinette.

"I'll tell her she must obey the fifth and sixth formers," she said. "But Angela, don't go too far, please. Most of us know that you are using your power too much in that direction."

"What about Mirabel?" said Angela, at once. "Doesn't she throw *her* weight about too much? She's unbearable this term, just because she's sports captain!"

"There's no need to discuss Mirabel," said Hilary. "What we've all got to realize this term, the term before we go up into the sixth, is that this is the form where we first shoulder responsibilities, and first have a little power over others. You're not given power to play about with and get pleasure from, Angela, as *you* seem to think. You're given it to use in the right way."

"Don't be so preachy," said Angela. "Really, are we never going to have any fun or good times again at St. Clare's? Every one looks so serious and solemn nowadays. Bobby and Janet never play tricks in class. We never have a midnight feast. We never . . ."

"Remember that we are all working jolly hard," said

41

Hilary, walking off. "You can't work hard and play the fool too. Wait till the exam. is over and then maybe we can have a bit of fun."

Hilary spoke to Antoinette and the small, dark-eyed French girl listened with the utmost politeness.

"Yes, Hilary, I will go to Angela when she sends for me," said Antoinette. "But always she send for me at so – busy a time!"

"Well, make your excuses to me, not to Angela," said Hilary, firmly. Antoinette looked at Hilary and sighed. She knew that Hilary would not believe in her excuses, and would insist, in that firm, polite way of hers, that Antoinette should do as she was told.

Angela saw Hilary speaking to Antoinette and was pleased. She decided to give Antoinette a bad time – she would teach her to "toe the mark" properly.

"Violet, I shan't want you for a few days," she told the adoring Violet. "Send me Antoinette instead."

"Oh, but Angela – don't I do your jobs well enough for you?" said Violet in dismay. "Antoinette is such a mutt – she can't do a thing! Really she can't. Let *me* do everything."

"Antoinette can sew and darn beautifully," said Angela, taking pleasure in hurting Violet, who had been very silly that week. "You made an awful darn in one of my tennis socks."

Violet's eyes filled with tears and she went out of the room. Alison looked up from her work.

"Angela, stop it," she said. "I think you're beastly – making the kids adore you and then being unkind to them. Anyway – you'll have a hard nut to crack in Antoinette! *She* won't adore you. She's got her head screwed on all right."

"She would adore me if I wanted her to," boasted Angela, who knew the power of her prettiness and smiles, and who could turn on charm like water out of a tap.

"She wouldn't," said Alison. "She's like Claudine – sees through every one at once, and sizes them up and then goes

42

her own way entirely, liking or disliking just as she pleases."

"I bet I'll make Antoinette like me as much as any of those silly kids," said Angela. "You watch and see. You'll be surprised, Alison."

"I'll watch – but I shan't be surprised," said Alison. "I know little Antoinette better than you do!"

Antoinette Defeats Angela

The next time she was sent for, Antoinette arrived promptly, all smiles. She was just as neat and chic as Claudine, quick-witted and most innocent-looking. Miss Jenks, the second form mistress, had already learnt that Antoinette's innocent look was not to be trusted. The more innocent she looked, the more likely it was that she had misbehaved or was going to misbehave!

"You sent for me, Angela?" said Antoinette.

"Yes," said Angela, putting on one of her flashing smiles. "I did. Antoinette, will you clean those brown shoes over there, please? I'm sure you'll do it beautifully."

Antoinette stared at Angela's beaming smile and smiled back. Angela felt sure she could see intense admiration in her eyes.

"The polish, please?" said Antoinette, politely.

"You'll find it in the cupboard, top shelf," said Angela. "How chic and smart you always look, Antoinette – just like Claudine."

"Ah, Claudine, is she not wonderful?" said Antoinette. "Angela, I have five sisters, and I like them all, but Claudine is my favourite. Ah, Claudine – I could tell you things about Claudine that would make you marvel, that would make you wish that you too had such a sister, and . . ."

But Angela was not in the least interested to hear what a

43

wonderful sister Claudine was, and she was certain she would never wish she had one like her. Angela preferred being a spoilt only child. You had to share things with sisters!

"Er – the polish is in the cupboard, top shelf," she said, her bright smile fading a little.

"The polish – ah yes," said Antoinette, taking a step towards the cupboard, but only a step. "Now, Claudine is not the only wonderful sister I have – there is Louise. Ah, I wish I could tell you what Louise is like. Louise can do every embroidery stitch there is, and when she was nine, she won . . ."

"Better get on with my shoes, Antoinette," said Angela, beginning to lose patience. A hurt look came into Antoinette's eyes, and Angela made haste to bestow her brilliant smile on her again. Antoinette at once cheered up and took another step towards the cupboard.

She opened her mouth, plainly to go on with her praise of Louise or some other sister, but Angela picked up a book and pretended to be absorbed in it.

"Don't talk for a bit," she said to Antoinette. "I've got to learn something."

Antoinette went to the cupboard. She took a chair and stood on it to get the polish. Then she stepped down with a small pot in her hand, and a little secret smile on her mouth – the kind of smile that Claudine sometimes wore. Angela did not see it.

Antoinette found a brush and duster and set herself to her task. She squeezed cream on to the shoes and smeared it on well. Then she brushed it in and then rubbed hard with the soft duster. She held the pair of shoes away from her and looked at them with pride.

"Done?" said Angela, still not looking up in case Antoinette began talking again.

"They are finished," said Antoinette. "Shall I clean yet another pair, Angela? It is a pleasure to work for you."

Angela was delighted to hear this. Aha – Alison would soon see that she could win the heart of Antoinette as easily as any one else's.

44

"Yes, Antoinette – clean all the shoes you like," she said. smiling sweetly. "How beautiful that pair look!"

"Do they not?" said Antoinette. "Such beautiful shoes they are too! Ah, no girl in the school wears such fine clothes as you, Angela – so beautifully made, so carefully finished. You have more chic than any English girl – you might be a Parisian!"

"I've been to Paris and bought clothes there two or three times," said Angela, and was just about to describe all the clothes when Antoinette started off again.

"Ah, clothes – now you should see my sister Jeanne! Such marvellous clothes she has, like those in the shops at Paris – but all of them she makes herself with her clever fingers. Such style, such chic, such . . ."

"You seem to have got a whole lot of very clever sisters," said Angela, sarcastically, but Antoinette did not seem to realize that Angela was being cutting.

"It is true," she said. "I have not yet told you about Marie. Now Marie . . ."

"Antoinette, finish the shoes and let me get on with my work," said Angela, who felt that she could not bear to hear about another sister of Antoinette's. "There's a good girl!"

She used her most charming tone, and Antoinette beamed. "Yes, Angela, yes. I am too much of a chattertin, am I not?"

"Box, not tin," said Angela. "Now, do get on, Antoinette. It's lovely to hear your chatter, but I really have got work to do."

Antoinette said no more but busied herself with three more pairs of shoes. She stood them in the corner and put the empty pot of cream into the waste-paper basket. "I have finished, Angela," she said. "I go now. Tomorrow you will want me, is it not so?"

"Yes, come tomorrow at the same time," said Angela, switching on a charming smile again and shaking back her gleaming hair. "You've done my shoes beautifully. Thank you."

Antoinette slipped out of the room like a mouse. She met

Claudine at the end of the passage and her sister raised her eyebrows. "Where have you been, Antoinette? You are not supposed to be in the fifth form studies unless you have been sent for."

"I have been cleaning all Angela's shoes," said Antoinette, demurely. Then she glanced swiftly up and down the corridor to see that no one else was in sight, and shot out a few sentences in rapid French. Claudine laughed her infectious laugh, and pretended to box her sister's ears.

"Tiens! Quelle mèchante fille! What will Angela say?"

Antoinette shrugged her shoulders, grinned and disappeared. Claudine went on her way, and paused outside Angela's study. She heard voices. Alison was there now too. Claudine opened the door.

"Hallo," said Alison. "Come for that book I promised you? Wait a minute – I've put it out for you somewhere."

She caught sight of all Angela's shoes standing gleaming in a corner. "I say! Did young Violet clean them like that for you? She doesn't usually get such a polish on!"

"No – Antoinette did them," said Angela. "She was telling me all about your sisters and hers, Claudine."

"Ah yes, said Claudine, "there is my sister Louise, and my sister Marie and my sister . . ."

"Oh, don't *you* start on them, for goodness' sake," said Angela. "What's the matter, Alison, what are you staring at?"

"Have you used up all that lovely face-cream al*ready*?" said Alison, in a surprised voice, and she picked an empty pot out of the waste-paper basket. "Angela, how extravagant of you! Why, there was hardly any out of it yesterday – and now it's all gone. What *have* you done with it?"

"Nothing," said Angela, startled. "I hardly ever use that, it's so terribly expensive and difficult to get. I keep it for very special occasions. Whatever can have happened to it? It really is empty!"

The two girls stared at each other, puzzled. Claudine sat on the side of the table, swinging her foot, her face quite impassive. Then Angela slapped the table hard and exclaimed in anger.

"It's that fool of an Antoinette! She's cleaned my shoes with my best face-cream! Oh, the idiot! All that lovely cream gone – gone on my shoes too!"

"But your shoes, they look so beautiful!" remarked Claudine. "Maybe the little Antoinette thought that ordinary shoe-polish was not good enough for such fine shoes."

"She's an idiot," said Angela. "I won't have her do any jobs again."

"Perhaps that's why she did this," said Alison, dryly. "It's the kind of thing our dear Claudine would do, for the same kind of reason, isn't it, Claudine?"

"Shall I tell Antoinette you will not need her again because you are very angry at her foolishness?" said Claudine. "Ah, she will be so sad, the poor child!"

Angela debated. She felt sure that Antoinette had made a real mistake. She was certain the girl liked her too much to play such a trick on her. How thrilled Antoinette had seemed when she had smiled at her! No – the girl had made a genuine mistake. Angela would give her another chance.

"I'll try her again," she said. "I'll forgive her this time. We all make mistakes sometimes."

"How true!" said Claudine. "Now, my sister Marie, hardly ever does she make a mistake, but once . . ."

"Oh, get out," said Angela, rudely. "It's bad enough to have you and Antoinette here without having to hear about your dozens of sisters!"

Claudine removed herself gracefully and went to find Antoinette to report the success of her trick. Antoinette grinned. *"C'est bien,"* she said. "Very good! Another time I will again be foolish, oh so foolish!"

Angela sent for her again the next day. Antoinette entered with drooping head and downcast eyes.

"Oh, Angela," she said, in a low, meek voice, "My sister Claudine has told me what a terrible mistake I made yesterday. How could I have been so foolish? I pray you to forgive me."

"All right," said Angela. "Don't look so miserable,

47

Antoinette. By the way, I think I'll call you Toni – it's so much friendlier than Antoinette, isn't it?"

Antoinette appeared to greet this idea with rapture. Angela beamed. How easy it was to get round these young ones! Well – she would get all the work she could out of this silly French girl, she would wind her round her little finger – and then she would send her packing and teach her a good sharp lesson!

"What would you have me do today?" Antoinette asked, in her meek voice. "More shoes?"

"No," said Angela. "No more shoes. Make me some anchovy toast, Toni."

"Please?" said Antoinette, not understanding.

"Oh, dear – don't you know what anchovy toast is?" sighed Angela. "Well, you make ordinary buttered toast – and for goodness' sake toast the bread before you put the butter on – then you spread it with anchovy paste. You'll find it in the cupboard. Make enough for three people. Anne-Marie is coming to tea, to read us her new poem."

"Ah, the wonderful Anne-Marie!" said Antoinette, getting out the bread. "Now one of my sisters, the one called Louise, once she wrote a poem and . . ."

"Toni, I've got to go and see some one," said Angela, getting up hurriedly. "Get on with the toast, and do it really carefully, to make up for your silly mistake yesterday."

"Angela, believe me, your little Toni will give you such toast as never you have had before!" said Antoinette with fervour. She held a piece of bread to the fire.

Angela went out, determined not to come back till Antoinette had made the toast and was safely out of the way. Talk about a chatterbox! She seemed to have a never-ending flow of conversation about her family. She might start on her brothers next – if she had any!

As soon as Angela had gone out of the room, Antoinette put aside her artless ways and concentrated on her job. She made six pieces of toast very rapidly and spread them with butter. Then she got a pot down from the cupboard shelf –

but it was not anchovy. It was the pot of brown shoe polish that she should have used the day before!

It looked exactly like anchovy as she spread it on the toast. Carefully the little monkey spread the brown paste, piled the slices on a plate and set them beside the fire to keep warm. Then she slipped out of the room and made her way to the noisy common room of her own form.

Soon Alison came in and sat down by the fire. Then Angela popped her head round the door and saw to her relief that Antoinette was gone.

"I simply couldn't stay in the room with that awful chatterbox, drivelling on about her sisters," said Angela. "Ah, she's made a nice lot of toast, hasn't she? Hallo – here's Anne-Marie."

Anne-Marie came in, her big eyes dark in her pale face. "You look tired," said Angela. "Been burning the midnight oil? I wish *I* could write poems like you, Anne-Marie."

"I worked on a poem till past twelve," said Anne-Marie, in her intense voice. "It's a good thing no one saw the light in my study. Ah – tea's ready, how lovely! Let's tuck in, and then I'll read my latest poem."

Three Disgusted Girls

Angela lifted the roast on to the table. "I got Antoinette to make anchovy toast for us," she said. "It looks good, doesn't it? Take a slice, Anne-Marie."

Anne-Marie took the top slice. It seemed to have rather a peculiar smell. Anne-Marie looked rather doubtfully at it.

"It's all right," said Alison, seeing her look. "Anchovy always smells a bit funny, I think."

She and Anne-Marie took a good bite out of their toast at the same second. The shoe-cream tasted abominable. Anne-Marie spat her mouthful out at once, all over the table. Alison, with better manners, spat hers into her handkerchief. Angela took a bite before she realized what the others were doing.

Then she too spat out at once, and clutched her mouth with her hands. "Oh! Oh! What is it? I'm poisoned!"

She rushed to the nearest bathroom and the others followed, their tongues hanging out. Anne-Marie was promptly sick when she reached the bathroom. Tears poured from her eyes and she had to sit down.

"Angela! What filthy paste? How *could* you buy such stuff?" she said.

"Horrible!" said Alison, rinsing her mouth out over and over again. "All that toast wasted too. It's wicked. Angela whatever possessed you to get paste like that? I've never tasted anchovy like that before, and I hope I never shall again. Ugh!"

Angela was feeling ill and very angry. What in the world had that idiot Antoinette done? They went back to the study and Angela opened the door of the little cupboard. She took down the pot of anchovy. It was untouched. So Antoinette couldn't have used it. Then what *had* she used? There was only jam besides the paste.

Alison picked up the pot of brown shoe-cream and opened that. It was practically empty. "Look," said Alison, angrily. "She used the shoe-cream – plastered all the toast with it! She deserves a good spanking."

Angela was white with anger. She put her head out of the door and saw a first former passing. "Hey, Molly," she called, "go and find Antoinette and tell her to come here at once."

"Yes, Angela," said Molly, and went off. Very soon Antoinette appeared, her dark eyes wide with alarm, and her lips trembling as if with emotion.

"Antoinette! How *dare* you put shoe-cream on our toast?" almost screamed Angela. "You might have poisoned us all. Can't you tell the difference between anchovy paste and shoe-polish, you absolute idiot? You've made us all ill. Matron will probably hear about it. You ought to be reported to Miss Jenks, you ought to . . ."

Anne-Marie rushed into the bathroom

"Ah, ah, do not scold your little Toni so," said Antoinette. "You have been so kind to me, Angela, you have smiled, you have called me Toni! Do not scold me so! I will give up my tea-time, I will make you more toast, and this time I will spread it with the anchovy, there shall be no mistake this time."

"If you think I'm ever going to trust you to do a single thing for me again, you're mistaken," said Angela, still tasting the awful taste of shoe-cream in her mouth. "I might have known a French girl would play the fool like this. I tell you, you've made us all ill. Anne-Marie was sick."

"I am desolated," wailed Antoinette. "Ah, Angela, I pray you to let me come again tomorrow. Tomorrow I will be so good, so good. Tomorrow you will call me Toni and smile at me again, tomorrow . . ."

"Tomorrow I'll get Violet Hill," said Angela. "Clear out, Antoinette, you're a perfect menace."

Antoinette cleared out and there was peace. "Well," said Angela, "she'll wish she'd been more sensible tomorrow. Serves her right! I was nice to her, and she thought the world of me – but I can't put up with idiots. She'll be jolly sorry when she sees I don't mean to give her another chance!"

"I don't feel like any tea now," said Alison, looking at the remains of the toast with dislike. "Do you, Anne-Marie?"

"No," said Anne-Marie, and shuddered. "I still feel sick. I don't even know if I can read my poem. It doesn't go very well with shoe-polish."

"Oh, do read it, Anne-Marie," begged Angela, who really did admire her poems. "What's it about?"

"It's all about the sadness of spring," said Anne-Marie, reaching for her poem. "It's a very sad poem, really."

"All your poems are sad," said Alison. "Why are they, Anne-Marie? I like poems that make me feel happy."

"I am not a very happy person," said Anne-Marie, very solemnly, and looked intense. "Poets aren't, you know."

"But some must have been," objected Alison. "I know lots of cheerful poems."

"Shut up, Alison," said Angela. "Read your poem, Anne-Marie."

Anne-Marie began her poem. It was very doleful, full of impressive words, and rather dull. Neither Alison nor Angela liked it very much, but they couldn't help feeling impressed. However could Anne-Marie write like that? She must indeed be a genius!

"It must be nice for you, sharing a study with Felicity, who thinks as much of music as you do of poetry," said Alison. "You ought to get Felicity to set some of your poems to music. That would be wonderful."

"I've asked her. She won't," said Anne-Marie. shortly. The truth was that Felicity would not admit that Anne-Marie's poems were worth tuppence. It was very humiliating to Anne-Marie.

"Write something real, and I'll put a tune to it," Felicity had said. "I'm not going to waste my music on second-rate stuff."

The door opened suddenly and Matron looked in. "I hear you poor girls have had a nasty dose of shoe-polish," she said. "I hope it wasn't anything very serious."

Angela thought she would take the chance of getting Antoinette into trouble, so she exaggerated at once.

"Oh, Matron, it was awful! We had our mouths absolutely full of the beastly stuff. Anne-Marie must have swallowed a lot, because she was sick. I shouldn't be surprised if we are ill, seriously ill tonight," said Angela.

"I'm sure I swallowed some," said Anne-Marie, looking solemn. "I expect we all did."

"Then you must come and have a dose at once," said Matron. "That shoe-cream contains a poisonous ingredient which may irritate your insides for a week or more, unless I give you a dose to get rid of it. Come along with me straight-away."

The three girls stared at her in alarm. They simply could not bear Matron's medicines. They were really so very nasty! Angela wished fervently that she had not exaggerated so much.

She tried to take back what she had said. "Oh well, Matron," she said, with a little laugh, "it wasn't as bad as all that, you know. We spat out practically all of it – and we rinsed our mouths out at once. We're *per*fectly all right now."

"I dare say," said Matron. "But I'd rather be on the safe side. I don't want you in bed for a week with a tummy upset of some sort. Come along. I've got something that will stop any trouble immediately."

"But Matron," began Alison.

It was no good. Nobody could reason with Matron once she had really decided to give any one a dose. The three girls had to get up and follow her. They looked very blue, and felt most humiliated. As a rule Matron left the fifth and sixth formers to look after themselves, and seldom came after them, suggesting medicine. They felt like first or second formers, trooping after her for a dose.

Matron took them to her room, and measured out the medicine into table-spoons, one for each of them. It tasted almost as nasty as the shoe-polish toast!

"Pooh!" said Alison, trying to get the taste out of her mouth. "Why don't you get some nice-tasting medicines, Matron? I've never tasted any so beastly as yours."

"Well, I've got a much worse one here," said Matron. "Would you just like to try it?"

"Of course not!" said Alison. Then a thought struck her. "Matron – how did you know we'd had shoe-polish on our toast today? We hadn't told a soul. Who told you?"

"Why, the poor little Antoinette told me," said Matron, corking up the bottle. "Poor child, she came to me in a terrible state, saying she had poisoned you all by mistake, and what was she to do if you died in the night, and couldn't I do something about it?"

The three girls listened to this with mixed feelings. So it was Antoinette who not only provided them with shoe-polish toast, but also with medicine from Matron! The little horror!

"You've no idea how upset she was," went on Matron, briskly. "Poor little soul, I felt really sorry for her. An English girl might have been amused at the mistake she had made, but Antoinette was so upset I had to comfort her and give her some chocolate. It's wonderful what chocolate will do to soothe the nerves of a first or second former! Nothing but babies, really."

The thought of Antoinette eating Matron's chocolate was too much for Angela, Alison and Anne-Marie. They felt that they simply *must* get hold of Antoinette and tell her what they thought of her.

"Where is Antoinete, do you know, Matron?" asked Angela, wishing she could get the combined taste of shoe-polish and medicine out of her mouth.

"I sent her to her aunt, Mam'zelle," said Matron, "I'm sure she would cheer her up and make her think she hadn't done such a dreadful thing after all! Fancy thinking she really had poisoned you!"

The three fifth-formers went back to the study. It wouldn't be a bit of good going to fetch Antoinette now. She would probably be having a nice cosy tea with Mam'zelle, who would be fussing her up and telling her everything was all right, a mistake was a mistake, and not to worry, *pauvre petite* Antoinette!

"I'll send for her tomorrow and jolly well keep her nose to the grindstone," said Angela, angrily. "I told her she needn't do anything more for me – but I'll make her now. I'll make her sorry she ever played those tricks. Clever little beast – going off to Matron and play-acting like that. She's worse than Claudine!"

Alison was alarmed to hear that Angela was going to make Antoinette do some more jobs for them.

"For goodness' sake, don't be silly!" she said to Angela. "Antoinette is far too clever for us to get even with. She'll only do something even worse than she has already done. I told you she wouldn't be like the others, silly and worship-ping. I told you she would size you up! I told you. . . ."

"Shut up, Alison," said Angela. "I hate people who say

'I told you, I told you!' I won't have Antoinette if you think she'll play worse tricks. She'd end in poisoning us, I should think. I wish I could pay her out, though."

"It's partly your own fault, all this," said Alison. "If only you'd treat the younger ones like the others do, sensibly and properly, we shouldn't have all these upsets."

Anne-Marie thought it was time to go. She always said that quarrels upset her poetic feelings. So she went, taking her mournful poem with her.

"We'd better not say a word about this to anyone," said Angela. "Else the whole school will be laughing at us. We won't let it go any further."

But alas for their plans – Antoinette told the story to everyone, and soon the whole school was enjoying the joke. It made Angela furious, for she hated being laughed at, it humiliated Alison too, for even Miss Willcox got to hear of it and teased her and Anne-Marie.

"What about a little essay on 'Anchovy Sauce'," she said. "Poor Alison, poor Anne-Marie, what a shame!"

Miss Willcox is in a Bad Temper

Miss Willcox was in a bad temper. She had just had back from her publishers her second book of poems, with a polite note to say that they were not as good as the first ones, and they regretted they did not see their way to put them into book-form.

Miss Willcox had an excellent opinion of her own writings, just as Anne-Marie had of hers. Also she had boasted in advance of her second book of poems – and now it would not be published. She was disappointed, and, like many rather weak characters, her disappointment turned to resentment instead of to a determination to go on and do better.

So she went to her English class looking rather grim, and feeling that she could not stand any nonsense or bad work that morning.

As a whole, the class had been working really very well, for Miss Willcox's lessons were interesting. Alma Pudden had not been able to keep up with the class very well, and Doris could not learn by heart with any success unless she was allowed to act what she said. Felicity too was only really interested if the poem or plays aroused her sense of rhythm and music.

The girls were rather tired that morning. They had had a strenuous half-hour with the gym.-mistress, who, feeling rather brisk, had put them through a great many vigorous exercises. Then had come a very hard three-quarters of an hour over maths. and then the English lesson. The girls were feeling that they wanted to relax a little – but here was Miss Willcox demanding intense concentration and attention.

Carlotta let out an enormous yawn which drew Miss Willcox's wrath upon her. Then Claudine said she felt sick and please could she go out of the room?

"It is astonishing how many times you manage to feel sick when you want to miss some part of a lesson," said Miss Willcox, irritated. "Go straight to Matron, please, and tell her."

"I would rather not," said Claudine, politely. "I do not feel sick enough for that. I can be sick in here if you would rather I stayed for the lesson."

It looked as if Miss Willcox was going to overwhelm Claudine with her wrath, when Felicity made them all jump. She began to tattoo on her desk, swaying to and fro in ecstasy.

"La-di-la-di-la!" she sang, "oh, la-la-la-di-la!"

"Felicity! What in the world are you doing?" cried Miss Willcox, incensed with rage. Felicity took not the slightest notice. With eyes still closed, she continued her swaying, and her singing, at times thumping the desk to accent the rhythm.

"*Felicity!*" almost shouted Miss Willcox, one of her gold-topped pins falling out of her hair on to the desk. She didn't notice it. "Do you hear what I say? What has come over this class this morning."

57

Bobby gave Felicity a bang on the shoulder. Felicity opened her eyes with a start, and gazed round the room. She did not in the least seem to take in the fact that she was in class and that Miss Willcox was furious with her. She shut her eyes again and began swaying.

"She's music-mad," said Bobby. "She's in a kind of music-dream, Miss Willcox. I don't believe she can help it. Hie, Felicity!"

"She goes like this in our study at night, very often," said Anne-Marie. "I often think she does it on purpose. She always does it when I want to read one of my poems out loud."

"Jolly sensible of her," remarked Pat.

"La-di-la-di-la!" hummed Felicity. Miss Willcox stared at her very hard. She simply could not make out if the girl's actions were genuine or put on.

"Boom-di-boom, di-boom," finished Felicity and banged the desk hard. "Ah, I've got it at last!"

The girls laughed. Acting or not, it was very funny. Felicity beamed round. "I have it!" she said. "The melody I've had in my mind for the last two weeks. It goes like this – la-di-la-di-la . . ."

Now it was Miss Willcox's turn to bang on the desk. It was seldom that she really did lose her temper, for she considered that meant a loss of dignity, and Miss Willcox always liked to appear dignified and self-controlled. But really, Felicity was too much for any one!

"Leave the room," commanded Miss Willcox, her voice trembling with anger. "I won't have any one in my class playing the fool like this. You shouldn't have come up into the fifth form – you should have gone down into the third!"

"Go out of the room?" said Felicity, puzzled. "Why must I? I didn't mean to interrupt the lesson – I didn't do it on purpose. It came over me suddenly. Now I am quite all right."

"Leave the room," ordered Miss Willcox again. The girls were silent. It was almost unheard-of for a fifth form girl to be sent from the room. If Miss Theobald heard of it

58

there would be serious trouble for Felicity.

Felicity got up and walked out of the room as if she was in a dream. She looked puzzled and shocked. She stood outside the door and leaned against the wall. Her head ached. Then the new melody came back again into it and she began to sing it quietly. The sound came into the silent classroom.

"Anne-Marie, tell Felicity to go to her study, and to write out the whole of the act of the play she is now missing," said Miss Willcox. "I will not have this behaviour."

"Felicity thinks she's a genius," said Anne-Marie. "She's always acting like this."

"I didn't ask for any comment," said Miss Willcox. She always forgot to put on her deep, rather drawling voice, when she was in a temper, and her voice now sounded rather harsh and unpleasant.

Almost every one got into trouble that morning. Doris was scolded for not knowing her part in the play they were reading. Alma was hauled up for eating sweets, "like any silly little first former," said Miss Willcox in disgust, taking the bag away from the fat, unhappy Alma.

"Poor little Pudding!" whispered Pat to Isabel. "I believe eating is her only pleasure in life!"

"Pat! What did you say?" demanded Miss Willcox. Pat went red.

"Well – I can't very well tell you," she said, not wishing to repeat what she had said, and hurt Alma.

Miss Willcox at once felt certain that Pat had been saying something rude about *her*. "Miss games this afternoon and write out your part in the play instead," she snapped. Pat looked upset, but did not dare to argue with Miss Willcox in her present mood.

The girls grew nervous. Pauline dropped her books on the floor and made Miss Willcox jump. She got a few sharp words that made her squirm and look at the mistress with resentment. Bobby debated whether or not to cheer things up by making Miss Willcox and the class laugh but decided that nothing on earth would get a smile out of the mistress

59

that morning. Whatever could be wrong with her? She was not usually like this.

Only Alison and Anne-Marie gazed at her with admiration that morning. They both thought that their beloved Miss Willcox looked lovely with her dark soulful eyes flashing. A bit of Miss Willcox's hair came down and hung by her ear. Alison saw her feeling about for the pin that usually kept it up, and walked from her seat.

She picked up the pin that had dropped and put it on Miss Willcox's desk with one of her rather sweet smiles. Somehow the action and the smile soothed Miss Willcox.

"Thank you, Alison," she said, using the deep voice that always thrilled Anne-Marie and Alison. "You are always on hand to help!"

Anne-Marie felt jealous. She never liked it when Miss Willcox praised Alison in any way. She sat looking gloomy. The class was amused to see this little byplay.

After the reading of the play was finished, there were five minutes left. "Has any one found anything interesting to read?" asked Miss Willcox, who always encouraged the class to bring any poem they liked or to quote any prose lines they came across, which pleased them.

Apparently no one had. "We've been working too hard this week to read much," said Hilary. "We haven't time for anything till this awful exam. is over."

"Miss Willcox," said Anne-Marie, nervously smiling. "Could I read the class a poem of mine, please? I would so like to know if you like it."

Miss Willcox was not really in the mood to hear poems by any one, since her own had been sent back. But the class, thinking that they could sit back and have a little rest for five minutes, applauded Anne-Marie's suggestion loudly. Anne-Marie flushed with pleasure. She thought they were welcoming her poem. It didn't enter her silly little head that the girls wanted a rest, and wouldn't listen to a word of it.

"Well," said Miss Willcox, rather ungraciously, "you can read if you like, Anne-Marie."

Anne-Marie got a piece of paper out of her desk, covered

with her sprawling hand-writing, which was always far too big. She cleared her throat, and began, putting on a deep voice that was supposed to be a flattering imitation of Miss Willcox's own style.

> "The lonely mill
> Lost in the wreathing mists of time,
> Silent as years that are lost,
> Brooding . . ."

Nobody but Angela listened. The whole class was bored to tears by Anne-Marie's pretentious, solemn and insincere poetry. Anne-Marie let herself go, and her voice rang quite sonorously through the classroom.

But she was not allowed to finish it. Miss Willcox had listened in a state of irritation, and stopped her half-way through. The poem was plainly an imitation of one of her own poems, in the book she had had published, and of which the adoring Anne-Marie had bought a copy.

Her poem was called "The Deserted Farm", and the whole plan of it was much the same as Anne-Marie's, even to the ideas in the different verses. As an imitation it was very clever – but Anne-Marie had not meant it to be an imitation. She had thought she was writing a most original poem, and had not even realized that she had drawn on her memories of Miss Willcox's own poem.

"Stop," said the mistress, and Anne-Marie stopped, puzzled. She glanced at Miss Willcox, who was frowning.

"When you write something *really* original, something out of your own mind, something which isn't copied from *my* work or any one else's, I'll listen to it, Anne-Marie," said Miss Willcox, putting on her deep, drawling voice again.

"But Miss Willcox – I didn't copy it from anywhere," stammered Anne-Marie, horrified. "I – I only tried to model it on your own style, which I admire very much. I – I –"

Even if Anne-Marie's poem had been as good as one by Shakespeare, Miss Willcox would not have admired it that morning, when she was still smarting from the sending back of her own precious collection of poems.

61

"Don't make excuses," she said coldly. "If I were you I should tear the poem up. Now – there's the bell. Put your books together and go out for Break. Alison, you can stay and help me for a few moments. I want these papers put in order."

In tears poor Anne-Marie went out of the room – and with smiles Alison helped Miss Willcox. The other girls hurried out thankfully – what a nerve-racking English lesson it had been!

About Geniuses, Sport and Mending

"You weren't sick after all, Claudine," said Angela, rather maliciously, as they went out.

"It passed," said Claudine, airily. "Happily Felicity took Miss Willcox's attention, or I might have had to go to Matron."

"We'd better go and get Felicity out of her study," said Isabel to Pat. "I wonder if she's written out the act of that play. It's an awfully long one."

They went to Felicity's study. Anne-Marie was there, crying. She scowled at the others when they came in.

"Cheer up, silly," said Pat. "What does it matter what dear Deirdre says about your poem? I bet she's jealous, that's all!"

"You don't know anything about poetry," sniffed Anne-Marie. "I don't believe you heard a word of my poem, anyway."

"Quite right, I didn't," said Pat. "I'd listen if I understood what you were trying to say in your poems Anne-Marie, but it always seems to me as if you haven't got anything to *say*."

"You're all unkind to me," sobbed Anne-Marie, thoroughly upset by two things – the fact that her precious poem had been scoffed at, and that her adored Miss Willcox had snubbed her.

"Oh, don't be such a baby," said Pat, and turned to look at Felicity, who was writing feverishly in a corner, copying out the play in a nervous, very small handwriting.

"Bad luck, Felicity," said Pat. "Come on out now, though. Do you good to get a blow in the air this morning. You look awful."

"I don't know what happened to me in class today," said Felicity, raising her head for a minute. "You see, I've been working so hard on my music, and the tune I've been groping for suddenly came to me – and my mind just went after it, and I forgot everything else."

"It's because you're a genius," said Pat, kindly, for she liked Felicity, who put on no airs at all, and was not in the least conceited. "Geniuses always do funny unusual things, you know. They can't help it. They like working in the middle of the night, they go without food for days sometimes, they walk in their sleep, they are absent-minded – oh, they're not like ordinary people at all. So cheer up – you can't help being a genius. Personally, I think you're working too hard."

Anne-Marie listened to this sympathetic speech with sniffles and a disconcerted look. She thought herself just as much a genius as Felicity – but nobody ever talked to *her* like that. Nobody ever called her a genius, except Angela – and Angela really didn't know the difference between a nursery rhyme and a great poem! Life seemed very hard to poor Anne-Marie just then.

"Perhaps," thought Anne-Marie, suddenly, "perhaps if I do some queer things, like Felicity does, the girls will realize I'm a genius too. It's worth trying, anyway – so long as I don't get myself into a row. It's no good doing anything in Miss Willcox's class – after Felicity's performance it would be silly."

She cheered up a little and went out for Break. Felicity would not go out. She was intent on finishing the writing out of the play, so that she could once more give her mind freely to the music that seemed always all around her. Felicity was finding things very hard that term. The work

63

in the fifth form was more difficult than in the fourth, and there was the strain of the exam. to face. She was also working even harder at her music, and very often could not sleep at night.

Mirabel also was working very hard at the sports standard of the whole school. She wanted to raise the standard of the lacrosse so that even the fourth and third teams would win all their matches. What a feather it would be in her cap, if she did!

Gladys did not approve of all this intense drive for high efficiency in games and gym. and running practice. "You're trying to do too much too quickly," she said to Mirabel. "You'll get much better results if you go more slowly, Mirabel. Look at this practice list of yours for the first form. You'll make them all fed up with games if you insist on so much time being given to them."

"Do them good," said Mirabel, intent on the second form list. "These kids ought to be very grateful for the interest I take in them. That Jane Teal for instance – she is ten times better since she did what I told her and put in more practice. She's the best catcher in the first form."

"Well, you can drive people like Jane Teal, who always wants to do the best they can for any one they like," said Gladys, "but you can't drive every one. Some just get obstinate. I think you're not at all sensible with some of the fourth formers – and you really ought to know better than go after people like Carlotta and Angela and Claudine."

"I wish you wouldn't always find fault with me, Gladys," said Mirabel, impatiently. "You're quite different from what you used to be. You used to like being guided by me, you said I was the strong one, and you quite looked up to me."

"I know," said Gladys, "and I do now. I only wish I had half your strength of will and purpose, Mirabel. But as I accepted the post of vice-captain, which does bring with it the responsibility of sharing with you most of your decisions, I can't sit back and not say things I ought to say. I don't *want* to say them – I know you won't like some of them – but I'd be a very poor thing if I *didn't* say them."

Mirabel really was surprised at Gladys. Always she had been the leader of the two and Gladys had followed meekly and willingly. It was something new for Mirabel to find Gladys sticking up for her own ideas, and actually going against her sometimes! Mirabel should have admired her quiet friend for this, but instead, glorying in her position of sports captain, she only felt resentful.

"I mean to make St. Clare's the best sports school in the country," she said obstinately. "I shan't listen to any excuses of over-work or tiredness from any one. They'll just have to put as much into their games as they do into their school-work."

"Every one is not as big and strong as you are," said Gladys, looking at the huge, strapping girl. "I don't wonder you are going to train as a games-mistress. You're just cut out for it! You could take gym. and games the whole day long and then go for a ten-mile walk in the evening! But do, do remember, Mirabel, old thing, that youngsters like Jane Teal really haven't the strength to do all *you* do!"

Jane Teal had most conscientiously done all that Mirabel had asked her, for she was a loyal and hard-working girl. She felt proud when Mirabel told her that she was now the best at ball-catching in lacrosse in the whole of her big form.

But she had never stopped worrying about Angela, and she longed to make up the quarrel with her, and do things for her again. She sat in prep. and debated things in her mind. How could she become friends with Angela again? How could she do her jobs instead of Violet, who, after the upset with Antoinette, had been taken back into favour again. She could not for the life of her think how to get back into Angela's good books.

"You seem to be lost in dreams, Jane," said Miss Roberts's voice. "I can't think you are doing your maths., with that faraway expression on your face."

"I – I was just thinking of something," said Jane, embarassed, and bent her head to her work.

The next day Violet went down with a very bad cold,

and was taken off to the san. by Matron, sniffling and feeling very sorry for herself. She called to Jane as she went.

"Find that school-story for me, and my new jig-saw puzzle and bring them in sometime to me," she said, and Jane promised she would. Accordingly she went to Violet's locker after morning school, and looked for the things she wanted.

She found them – and she also found two pairs of Angela's stockings and two vests, all wanting quite a lot of mending. She stared at them.

Violet would be away from school for three or four days. Should she, Jane, do the mending, and take it back to Angela, and ask if she might take Violet's place till she came back! It would be lovely to go to her study again, and tidy up the beautiful place, look at the pictures on the wall, fill the vases with water – do all the things she loved doing. Angela would smile at her again, and everything would be all right.

Jane mended everything beautifully, spending all her free time on the stockings and the vests. Some of her free time should have been spent in learning a part in a play the first form were doing. How could she learn it, when she had to go to bed early, like all the other first formers?

"I'll take my torch to bed with me, and when the others are asleep, I'll switch it on under the bed-clothes and learn my part then," thought Jane. She was pleased at having thought of such a good way out. No one would know. She did not think of how tired she would feel the next day!

She took the things to Angela that afternoon when Angela sent for Violet. She went in timidly, her heart beating fast, for she was afraid of Angela's sneers and snubs.

Alison was there alone. She was surprised to see Jane. "Hallo, kid," she said. "Where's Violet?"

"In the san. with a cold," said Jane. "I mended Angela's things instead. Where is she, Alison?"

"Having a talk with Mirabel," said Alison. Mirabel had been having serious talks with all the fifth form that day, asking them to help her in making the sports standard for

St. Clare's much higher. She would certainly not have much success with Angela, who detested getting hot and untidy!

"Oh," said Jane, disappointed, and put the mended stockings and vests down. Then her face brightened, for Angela came into the room and shut the door violently. She looked cross.

"That idiot of a Mirabel!" she said to Alison, not seeing Jane at first. "She wants to turn us all into tomboys like herself, great strapping creatures, striding along instead of walking, shouting instead of speaking, playing . . ."

"Jane is here," said Alison, warningly. Angela turned and saw her. She still looked cross, and Jane hastened to explain why she was there.

"Violet's ill, please Angela," she said. "So I have done your mending myself. I hope you don't mind. I – I – would like to do it for you again, if you'll let me."

Angela stared at Jane unsmilingly. "But what about dear Mirabel, and her anxiety to make you into a wonderful little sportswoman?" she said in a mocking voice.

"I can do both," said Jane, anxiously. "I can make time for my work, and my games and for anything you'd like me to do too."

Angela knew it would annoy Mirabel if she heard that she was making Jane spend her time on all kinds of jobs for her. So she nodded her head and gave the girl a slight smile, which was heaven to Jane.

"All right," she said. "I'll have you again. I'm tired of that silly Violet anyway, with her big cow's-eyes. You can come instead."

Filled with delight Jane sped off. Everything was all right again! The wonderful Angela had smiled at her! She didn't mind if she had to work in bed every night so long as Angela went on being nice to her.

Mirabel Makes Herself A Nuisance

Mirabel was really making herself a nuisance just then, especially with the fifth form, who were working very hard indeed for the exam. She was trying to get them interested in the younger ones, to make them go and take practice games with them. They objected to this very much.

"It's a silly idea," said Pat. "Those babies much prefer to practise on their own. They don't like being chivvied about by us big ones."

"Besides, we've got to *work*," said Hilary, exasperated. "I can't imagine when you do any extra work for the exam., Mirabel – I'm sure you spend all your evenings in your study, preparing your sports lists and list for matches, and goodness knows what."

It was true that Mirabel was doing very little extra work. She was trusting to scrape through the exam., but she did not care whether she got good marks or not. Her whole soul was in the running of the school games, and she often annoyed the games-mistress intensely. But Mirabel's thick skin made her quite invulnerable to cutting remarks or snubs.

"She just drives on like a tank," said Bobby. "Nobody can stop her. She'll have us all trailing after her helping her in her sports ideas just because we're so tired of arguing with her."

"You can't argue with Mirabel," said Doris. "She never listens to a word any one says. I doubt if she even listens to Gladys now. It's a pity Gladys isn't a stronger character. She might have some influence over our head-strong Mirabel!"

"Gladys *used* to have influence over her," said Pat. "Do you remember when Mirabel first came to St. Clare's and was rude and defiant, and said she wouldn't stay longer than half-term, whatever happened?"

"Yes," said Isabel, remembering. "She was simply unbearable – quite unreasonable. And it was the little Mouse Gladys, who got her round, and made her stay on, and become quite a decent member of St. Clare's."

"But Mirabel has got swelled-head now she's sports captain," said Bobby. "Gladys can't do anything with her. I heard her arguing with Mirabel the other day, and all that happened was that Mirabel got angry and shut her up."

"I have never liked this Mirabel of yours," remarked Claudine, who had consistently got out of games and gym. whenever she could, all the time she had been at St. Clare's. "She is always hunting me here, there and everywhere, calling upon me to do this and that."

The girls smiled. Claudine usually found it quite easy to evade people who wanted her to do something she disliked, but few people were so persistent as Mirabel. No matter where Claudine hid herself Mirabel would run her to earth, produce a list of games and try to pin Claudine down to a practice.

"Yesterday, in my great despair, I went to speak to Miss Theobald," said Claudine, raising her eyebrows and her shoulders in an amusing way. "There was Mirabel close behind me, waving a great list, and there was I, taking to my toes."

"Heels," said Bobby, laughing.

"I run fast," said Claudine, "and I find myself outside Miss Theobald's door. What shall I do to get away from this dreadful Mirabel? I knock at the door. I go in!"

The girls were amused and wondered what Claudine could have found so suddenly to say to Miss Theobald.

"What excuse did you make?" asked Janet.

"I held a long conversation with Miss Theobald," said Claudine, solemnly. "Ah, we talked, and we talked, whilst the poor Mirabel, she waited patiently outside the door!"

"What on earth did you talk about?" said Bobby, curiously.

Claudine looked mischievous. "There was no Miss Theobald there!" she said. "I talked to myself, and then

I talked again as if I was answering. The door was shut. How could the good, patient Mirabel know that only I, Claudine, was in the room?"

"Was Mirabel outside the door when you went out?" said Bobby.

"Alas – Miss Theobald herself came to the door when Mirabel was standing there," said Claudine. "The poor Mirabel! She must have been so surprised to see Miss Theobald, as surprised as I was suddenly to hear her voice outside the door. Me, I did not stay in the room any longer. I jumped out of the window. The gardener was there, and he too jumped – how do you say it – he jumped out of his skin."

The girls yelled at the thought of Claudine jumping out of Miss Theobald's window, in order to avoid both Mirabel and Miss Theobald. None of the others, except perhaps Carlotta, would have thought of doing such a thing.

"You really are the limit," said Bobby.

"What is this 'limit' that you are always talking of?" inquired Claudine.

"Never mind. What happened next?" said Hilary, who always enjoyed Claudine's pranks.

"Ah, well – I went in at the side-door," said Claudine, "and I heard Miss Theobald and Mirabel being most surprised at each other. Miss Theobald said 'My dear Mirabel, how can Claudine be talking to me in the drawing-room if I am here, outside the door? Do not be foolish'."

The girls giggled. "Didn't Miss Theobald open the door?" asked Janet.

"Yes," said Claudine, "and there was no one in the room. Ah, it was good to see poor Mirabel's face then! So surprised it was, so puzzled. And Miss Theobald, she was quite cross."

"Did Mirabel ask you what had happened?" said Pat, grinning.

"Ah yes – she asks me so many times," said Claudine. "And I say, 'I do not understand, Mirabel. Speak to me

70

Claudine jumped out of the window

in French.' But the poor Mirabel, her French is so bad I do not understand that either!' "

"Sh – here *is* Mirabel," said Pauline, as the sports captain came into the room. You always knew when Mirabel was coming – she walked heavily, she flung doors open, and her voice was loud and confident. She came towards the girls.

"I say," she said, "I've just got Miss Theobald's permission to call a big sports meeting tomorrow night in the assembly hall. Seven o'clock. It's to discuss all the matches this term – and there are some jolly important ones. Seven o'clock, don't forget. And I shall expect every member of the fifth form to be there. The younger girls are all coming, of course, and it wouldn't do to let them see any of us slacking or not attending the meeting."

"Yes, but Mirabel – it's Saturday night, and you know we were going to have a dance," protested Angela. "You *know* that. It was all arranged. The third and fourth form were coming too. It was to be real fun."

"Well, I put the meeting tomorrow night because the dance isn't a bit important and the meeting *is*," said Mirabel. "We can have a dance any other Saturday. But I've got quite a lot of new ideas to put before the school. I've been working them all out."

"You might ask *us* if we would agree to exchanging a dance for your silly meeting," said Alison. "You're so jolly high-handed! I shan't come to the meeting. I've got better things to do."

Mirabel looked shocked. How could there be better things to do than attend a sports meeting, and discuss the ins and outs of matches? She stared at Alison and frowned.

"You've got to come," she said. "Miss Theobald said I could arrange the meeting, and tell every one to attend. It won't take long."

"You always say that – but your meetings take hours," said Carlotta. "You stand up and talk and talk and talk. I shan't come."

"I shall report any one who doesn't," said Mirabel, beginning to look angry.

"Mirabel – put the meeting another time," said Hilary. "You're only getting every one's back up. You really are. We want a little fun tomorrow night. We've all worked hard this week."

"I'm sorry," said Mirabel, stiffly. "The meeting will be held tomorrow night, and nothing will prevent it, not even *your* wish, my dear Hilary. You may be head of the form, but I am head of the whole school for sports."

She went out and shut the door loudly. She knew the girls would say hard things about her, but she didn't care. She meant to have her way. The girls would thank her all right when every single match against other schools was won! She would put St. Clare's at the top.

"She has a wasp in her hat, that girl," said Claudine, disgusted.

"A bee in her bonnet, you mean," said Pat. "How you do get things mixed up, Claudine! Yes, old Mirabel certainly has got a bee in her bonnet – it's sports, sports, sports with all her all the time, and every one else has got to be dragged into it too. I love games – but honestly, I find myself not wanting to turn out on the field now, simply because I know Mirabel will be there, ready to check all shirkers and late-comers!"

"Shall we *have* to go to this beastly boring meeting?" said Felicity. "I wanted to work at my music."

"And I wanted to finish my new poem," said Anne-Marie at once.

"We'll have to go, if Miss Theobald has agreed to let Mirabel call the meeting," said Hilary, reluctantly. "I suppose she told Miss Theobald that we were all keen on the meeting. It's a nuisance – but we'll have to turn up."

"Maybe the meeting will not be held after all," said Claudine.

"Not a hope," said Bobby. "I know Mirabel. Once she makes up her mind about something, that something hap-

73

pens. She's a born dictator. She'll be appalling in the sixth form!"

"I think maybe the meeting will not happen after all," said Claudine, looking dreamily into space.

"What do you mean?" said Bobby.

"I have a feeling here," said Claudine, pressing a hand to her tummy. "It tells me, this feeling, that something will stop the meeting tomorrow night. What can it be?"

Hilary looked suspiciously at Claudine, who was wearing one of her most innocent and angelic expressions. Claudine returned her look with candid wide-open eyes.

"Are you planning anything?" said Hilary. "Because if so, don't. You can't meddle with things like school meetings, once you're a fifth former."

"How true!" said Claudine, with a sigh, and went off to her study with Carlotta.

That night, when every one in Claudine's room was asleep the little French girl slipped out of bed and went along the corridor. She went down the stairs and soon returned with something that shone brightly each time she passed under a dimmed light. She deposited it in an unused chest outside the dormitory door, covered it with an old rug, and then slipped along another corridor to the dormitory in which her sister Antoinette slept.

She awoke Antoinette by a light touch, and knelt by her sister's bed to whisper.

"*Oui, oui*," whispered back Antoinette, "yes! Yes, Claudine, I will do as you say. Do not fear. It will be done!"

Claudine slipped back to bed like a little white ghost. She climbed between the sheets, grinning to herself. Dear Mirabel, it will be difficult for you to hold your meeting tomorrow, poor Mirabel, you will be disappointed, foolish Mirabel, you cannot get the better of the little French Claudine! With these pleasant thoughts Claudine fell fast asleep.

The Meeting Is Spoilt

The third, fourth, and fifth forms were very much annoyed and upset by Mirabel's command to attend the sports meeting on Saturday night. They had looked forward to the dance so much – it was just like Mirabel to spoil everything!

"She walks about with those long strides of hers as if she owns the whole school," said Belinda of the fourth form.

"I used to like games but now I'm getting fed up with them," complained Rita of the third form. "Mirabel ticks me off in public on the field as if I were one of the first form. I won't stand it!"

But she did stand it because Mirabel was a very strong personality determined to get her own way. She was using her power to the utmost and beyond.

The fifth formers all put away their various occupations that Saturday night as seven o'clock drew near. They grumbled as they shut their books, rolled up their knitting, put away their letters. But not one of them refused to go when the time came, for they knew that, as fifth formers, they must turn up even if only as a good example to the younger ones.

Mirabel was standing on the platform of the assembly hall, running through the list of things she meant to say. She glanced up as the girls came filing in, her quick eyes watching to see that every one turned up. Woe betide any unlucky first or second former who did not arrive! Mirabel would be after them the next day!

Antoinette came up to Mirabel. The sports captain glanced up impatiently. "What is it, Antoinette?"

"Please, Mirabel, may the second form have a new ball to practise with?" said Antoinette. "It seems that we have lost the one we had, and we are oh, so keen, to practise hard for you."

"Hm," said Mirabel, rather disbelievingly, for Antoinette could not by any means have been called keen on games. "Why didn't Violet come to me about it?"

"Violet is in the san.," said Antoinette.

"Well, come to me on Monday about the ball. I can't possibly deal with matters like that now," said Mirabel. "You ought to know better than to come just before an important meeting like this."

"Yes, Mirabel," said Antoinette, and sidled away. Mirabel thought of her with exasperation. She was a slacker, just like Claudine – but she would pin her down and make her play games properly if it took her three terms to do it!

The girls all filed in. Mirabel caught sight of Jane Teal in the first-form benches, looking rather pale. Jane was gazing at Angela, who was looking very beautiful that evening. She had had her hair washed, and it glistened like finest gold. Mirabel frowned. She wished that Jane and the other first formers would stop raving about that foolish Angela!

She ran her eyes over the fifth form. They all seemed to be there – but wait a minute, where was Felicity?

Mirabel spoke to Anne-Marie, who was passing by the platform at that moment. "Where's Felicity?"

"She's coming, Mirabel," said Anne-Marie, shortly, for she, like every one else, resented giving up a jolly dance for a dull meeting. "She had some music to finish copying out. She said she was just coming."

"Well, I shall begin without her," said Mirabel. "She's always unpunctual. Such a bad example for the younger ones! It's a minute past seven already."

Every one was now in their seats. There was a great shuffling of feet, and an outbreak of coughing from the second form, who were a very lively lot this term.

Mirabel went to the front of the platform. She looked enormous there. She began very self-confidently, for she was seldom at a loss for words, when her beloved games were the subject.

76

"Good evening, girls," she began, in her loud, determined voice. "I have called this important meeting here to-night for a very special reason. I want to make St. Clare's the head of all the schools in the kingdom in their proficiency at games of all kinds. I want us to have hockey as well, I want us to . ."

Then came an interruption. A first-form girl stood up and stopped Mirabel.

"Jane isn't well. She says she won't leave the meeting, but she must, mustn't she?"

It was Sally, Jane Teal's friend. Every one turned to look at poor Jane, who, white in the face, felt quite faint with embarrassment.

"Take her out, Sally," said Mirabel, rather impatiently. She did not like being interrupted in her opening speech. Sally helped Jane out. "Are you going to be sick?" she asked in a loud whisper, which embarrassed poor Jane even more. She was terribly upset at holding up Mirabel's meeting, but she really did feel queer.

The two went out, and Mirabel resumed her speech, which went on for three or four minutes. "I want us to win all our lacrosse matches, I want us to form a hockey team that is unbeatable, I want us to . . ."

But what else Mirabel wanted nobody ever knew. There came a sudden and unusual noise that made every one jump violently. It was the loud clanging of the school fire-bell!

Clang! Clang! Clang! Clang!

Mirabel stopped and listened, startled. Fire! This was not just a practice alarm she was sure – Miss Theobald would never choose a time like this for an unexpected fire-practice; she knew there was an important meeting being held.

The first and second formers looked uneasily at one another, and then looked for a lead from the older ones. There were no mistresses present.

Hilary stood up, her face quite calm. "Help me to get the first and seconds out quietly," she said to the twins and to Janet and Bobby. "We'll march them into the grounds, out by the side door."

Mirabel also took quick command. Her strong voice rang out reassuringly.

"That's the school fire-bell. You all know what to do. Stand, please."

The girls stood, glad to have a leader. Mirabel saw that Hilary, the twins, Bobby and Janet had moved across to the younger girls, and she saw that she could expect the utmost help from them. Some of the first formers looked rather scared.

"Right turn!" roared Mirabel. "Follow Hilary Wentworth. *March!*"

In perfect order, without any panic at all, the first and second forms marched out, led by Hilary, who undid the garden door and went into the grounds. It was a dark night, but the girls knew the grounds well.

Pat and Isabel took out the second form. Bobby and Janet, and the head-girl of the third form then marched off with that form. The fourth formers followed with the fifth, sniffing the air eagerly to see if they could smell smoke.

"Where's the fire?" cried Belinda. "I can't see a sign anywhere!"

Mirabel went out of the hall last, pleased to find that she could handle an emergency so efficiently. Her loud confident voice had at once instilled trust into every girl. She wondered where the fire was.

The first of the mistresses to arrive on the scene was Mam'zelle. Miss Theobald was out, and the French Mistress had been left in charge for that evening. The loud, distressed voice of Mam'zelle was heard long before she appeared in the doorway.

"Ah! Where are the girls? Yes, yes – in the assembly hall. To think that a fire should come when Miss Theobald is out! Girls, where are you, Claudine, Antoinette, show yourselves to me, I pray you! Are you safe?"

"Quite safe!" came Claudine's amused voice, and then Antoinette left the darkness of the grounds and went to where Mam'zelle stood in the doorway. "I too am safe," she said in her demure voice.

Mam'zelle threw her arms round Antoinette as if she had rescued her from flames. "Ah, my little Antoinette! Do not be afraid. I am here, your strong Aunt Mathilde! "

"Where's the fire, Mam'zelle?" called a voice.

"Ah, the fire! Where is it?" repeated Mam'zelle, still feeling rather dazed.

Then Matron appeared on the scene, and took command at once. She had sped round the school immediately she had heard the fire-bell, to see where the fire could be. She had been to the place where the fire-bell was kept to see who was ringing it — but the fire-bell was standing in its place, and no one was near it!

She was puzzled, but as her nose, eyes and ears told her that certainly there was no fire raging anywhere near she felt sure that some one had been playing a joke. Matron had been long enough at St. Clare's to smell a joke a mile away by now.

"Girls, come in at once!" she said, in her crisp, cool voice. "There is no fire. But I must congratulate you on responding to the bell so quickly and quietly, and going out of doors in this sensible way."

"Well, we were all at a meeting," said Hilary, who was near the door. "It was easy. We just marched out. But Matron — who rang the bell then?"

"We shall no doubt find that out later," said Matron, dryly. "In the meantime, please march indoors again."

The girls all marched in. Some of them were shivering, for it was a cold night. Matron saw this and hoped the san. would not be inundated with people having colds the following week!

She looked at her watch and made up her mind quickly. "You will all go to your common rooms and your studies at once," she said. "Head-girls, make up the fires in the common rooms, please, and see that the rooms are warm. In ten minutes' time come to the kitchen, two girls from each form, and there will be jugs of hot cocoa ready, which

79

I want you all to drink as soon as possible."

This was pleasant news. The girls hurried in, glad to think of warm fires and hot cocoa. But Mirabel was annoyed. She spoke to Matron.

"Matron, I'm sorry, but I'm afraid the girls must go back to the hall. We were just beginning a most important meeting. Shall I tell them or will you?"

Matron looked hard at the self-confident Mirabel. "We shall neither of us tell them," she said. "You heard what I said to them. They've had a spell out there in the cold and I don't want them to get chills. There will be no meeting tonight."

"'Hurrah!'" said one or two low voices, as the girls hurrying in heard this welcome news. "Good old Matron."

Mirabel ought to have known that one person she could never flout was Matron. She began to argue. "But Matron – this is a most important meeting. I shall have to go to Miss Theobald, I'm afraid, and ask her for her authority to continue my meeting, if you won't give the girls permission."

"Very well. Go and ask her," said Matron, who knew quite well that Miss Theobald was out. So off went Mirabel, angry and determined, bitterly disappointed that her wonderful meeting was spoilt.

But Miss Theobald was not in her drawing-room. It was most annoying. Mirabel hardly dared to go back and take up the matter with Matron again. She had not at all liked the tone of Matron's voice. Her spirits sank and she felt rather miserable.

Then her face grew grim. "Well, I shall find out who rang that bell and spoilt my meeting, anyway! And won't I give them a dressing-down – in front of the whole school, too!"

Who Rang the Fire-bell?

Mirabel went storming to her study. Gladys was there, warming herself in front of a cheerful little fire.

"Pity the meeting was spoilt," she said, thinking that Mirabel would be in need of a little comfort about it. "You were making a very good speech, Mirabel."

"Gladys, who do you think rang that fire-bell?" said Mirabel, grimly. "Is that cocoa in the jug? I'll have a cup. Not that I'm cold, but I do feel a bit upset at having the meeting completely spoilt by some silly idiot who thinks it clever to play a practical joke like that."

Gladys said nothing. She had no idea at all who the culprit could be. Mirabel stirred her cocoa violently, and went on talking.

"Who wasn't there? Well, Felicity wasn't, of course! Gladys, could it have been Felicity?"

"Of course not," said Gladys. "I don't suppose Felicity even knows there is a fire-bell, let alone where it is!"

"Well – I shall certainly find out where she was all the time," said Mirabel. "This is really the sort of idiotic joke Claudine would play – but she was there all the time. I saw her myself – and Antoinette was there too, because she came up and spoke to me at the beginning of the meeting."

"And she was out in the grounds with the others," said Gladys, remembering. "Didn't you see her go up to Mam'zelle and speak to her when Mam'zelle yelled out for Claudine and Antoinette?"

"Yes," said Mirabel, frowning. "Well, who else wasn't there? Violet is in the san. Every one else was there as far as I can remember. I ticked people off as they came in, because I wasn't going to let any one get out of the meeting if I could help it."

Gladys offered no suggestion. Mirabel suddenly slapped

the table hard and made Gladys jump. "Don't, Mirabel," she said. "Don't be so violent."

Mirabel took no notice. "Of course – Jane Teal went out, didn't she – and Sally. Do you think either of them would have done it?"

"I shouldn't think so for a moment," said Gladys. "Why, Jane is very fond of you, and Sally is far too sensible to do a thing like that."

"I shall find out," said Mirabel, her face hard. Gladys looked rather distressed.

"Don't go about it too angrily," she said. "You'll only put people's backs up."

"I don't care if I do," said Mirabel, and she didn't. Gladys sighed. If only Mirabel did care a little more about other people's feelings, she would find them easier to tackle. She was always complaining that people would not co-operate with her or help her.

Mirabel gulped down her cocoa. "I'm going off to Felicity's study first," she said. "See you later."

She went out of the room. Gladys took up some knitting. She was making a jumper for her mother, and she had very little spare-time for it, with all her exam. work, sports work, and Mirabel's incessant demands to cope with. She couldn't help feeling rather glad that she had an unexpected hour to get on with her knitting!

Mirabel went into Felicity's study. Felicity was there, trying her violin softly, whilst Anne-Marie sat over the fire, a pencil and notebook on her knee, trying to compose a wonderful new poem. She kept frowning at Felicity's soft playing, but Felicity was quite unaware of Anne-Marie's frowns or even of Anne-Marie herself. She jumped violently when Mirabel came into the room.

Then, thinking she had come to see Anne-Marie, she went on with her soft playing. Mirabel spoke to her roughly.

"Felicity, why weren't you at the sports meeting this evening?"

Felicity looked startled. "Oh, Mirabel – I'm so sorry. I really did mean to come, and I forgot all about it! I was

82

playing my violin, and somehow forgot I had said I would go! How awful of me!"

"Where were you when the fire-bell went?" said Mirabel.

"Fire-bell?" said Felicity, looking astonished. "What fire-bell?"

"She never hears anything but her music when she's really wrapped up in it," said Anne-Marie. "You know how she behaved in class the other day, Mirabel. I don't expect she heard the bell at all."

"I didn't," said Felicity, looking really bewildered now. "Did it ring? Was there a fire? What happened?"

"Oh, you're hopeless," said Mirabel, and went out of the study. Felicity stared at Anne-Marie, who made an impatient noise, stuffed her fingers in her ears, and tried to go on with her poem.

Mirabel went to find Jane Teal and Sally. They were in the first-form common room, Jane still looking rather pale, but better. She flushed when Mirabel came in, quite thinking that the sports captain had come to see how she was.

But Mirabel hadn't. She came straight to the point. "Jane and Sally – did either of you ring the fire-bell when you left the meeting?"

The girls stared at her in surprise. It would not have occurred to either of them to spoil such an important meeting! Jane felt very hurt to think that Mirabel should imagine her to be capable of such a thing.

"Well – haven't either of you tongues?" said Mirabel. The whole of the first form had now gathered round the three, and were listening with the greatest interest.

"Of *course* we didn't," said Sally, indignantly. "As if we'd do a thing like that! Anyway, poor Jane was feeling awfully ill. She had a terrible headache. She's always having headaches."

"Shut up, Sally," said Jane, who knew that Mirabel did not look very kindly on such things as headaches.

"Did you leave Jane alone at all?" said Mirabel to Sally. "Yes – you came back to the meeting without her, didn't

83

you? Then she could easily have slipped out of your common room and rung the bell, couldn't she?"

"*Oh!*" said Sally, really indignant, "as if Jane would do a mean thing like that! Yes, I did leave her here as he seemed a bit better and I went back to the meeting – and as soon as I sat down, the bell rang. But it wasn't Jane ringing it."

Jane was terribly upset to think that Mirabel should even think she could spoil a meeting of hers. Her lips trembled, and she could not trust herself to speak.

"Now don't burst into tears like a baby," said Mirabel to Jane. "I'm not saying you *did* do it – I'm only saying that you had the *chance* to do it. It just puzzles me to know who could have done it, because everybody was at the meeting, except you and Felicity – and I'm pretty certain that Felicity didn't even know St. Clare's possessed such a thing as a fire-bell!"

"Well, it looks as if I must have done the deed then," said Jane, bitterly, trying to keep the tears out of her eyes. "Think it was me, if you like. I don't care!"

"Now that's not the way to talk to your sports captain," said Mirabel. "I'm surprised at you, Jane. Well, I suppose I shall find out one day who rang that bell."

She went out of the room and shut the door unnecessarily loudly. The first formers looked at one another.

"Beast," said Sally. "I shan't do one single minute's more lacrosse practice than I can help!"

"Nor shall I," said Hilda, and the others all agreed, Jane mopped her eyes, and the others comforted her.

"Never mind, Jane. Don't you worry about it. We all know you didn't do it!"

"I wish I knew who *had* done it," said Sally, her eyes sparkling. "I'd go and pat her on the back and say 'Jolly good show!'"

The others laughed and agreed. It was queer how in a few short weeks Mirabel had changed from an object of great admiration into one of detestation.

Miss Theobald had to be told about the strange ringing

of the fire-bell, apparently done by nobody at all. She was rather inclined to take a serious view of it and Mirabel was pleased.

"I am glad you too think it is a serious matter to have an important, pre-arranged meeting completely spoilt by somebody's stupid ragging," said Mirabel.

"Oh, dear me, I was not thinking of your meeting," was Miss Theobald's rather damping reply. "I was thinking that I cannot have the fire-bell rung without proper cause. If it is, then the girls will not take warning when the bell is rung for a real fire. That is a very serious matter – not the interruption of your meeting."

"Oh," said Mirabel, rather crest-fallen. "Well, could I have the meeting next Saturday night instead, Miss Theobald?"

"I'm afraid not," said the Head Mistress. "The heads of the third, fourth and fifth forms have already been to me to ask me if they may have the postponed dance then, Mirabel. I don't think we can possibly expect them to postpone it again. These forms are working very hard this term, and very well. I want them to relax when they can."

Mirabel left Miss Theobald, angry and depressed. She went into her study and sat down at the table to do some work. "What's the matter?" said Gladys.

"Hilary and the head-girls of the third and fourth have been to Miss Theobald behind my back and got her to say they could have their dance this coming Saturday," said Mirabel, gloomily. "It's absolutely the only chance I have of getting the whole school together on Saturday evenings, and they know it. Deceitful beasts!"

"Don't be silly," said Gladys, feeling a wave of anger. "They probably never even *imagined* you'd actually want them to give up *another* Saturday evening. Do be sensible, Mirabel. And look here – why have you left little Jane Teal out of next week's matches? She's very good and you know it. It will break her heart to be left out, when you've as good as told her she might play."

"I'm not satisfied that she didn't have something to do

with the ringing of that bell," said Mirabel.

"*Well!*" said Gladys, exasperated, "you might at least wait till you *are* sure, before you punish her like this. I think she's a very decent little kid, I must say, and I'm dead certain she wouldn't do a thing like that."

"Look here, *I'm* captain, not you!" said Mirabel, losing her temper. "I keep *on* having to remind you of that. I won't have you preaching at me and interfering."

Gladys went rather white. She hated rows of any sort, and always found it difficult to stand up to Mirabel for any length of time. She took up a book and said no more. Mirabel took up a book too, and looked at it frowning. But she did not see a word that was printed there. She was turning over and over in her mind the same question – WHO rang that fire-bell?

She would have been interested in a little conversation between Claudine and Antoinette if she could have heard it.

"Very good, *ma petite*," Claudine remarked to Antoinnette. "It was good to show yourself so well to Mirabel at the beginning of the meeting, and to appear out in the grounds when *Tante* Mathilde called us. There is no one who thinks of you, no one at all."

"Clang, clang, clang!" said Antoinette, her dark eyes gleaming with mischief. "I felt like the old town crier at home. Clang, clang, clang, the meeting will not be held, clang, clang, clang! Ah, it is a good bell to ring!"

"Sh. Here come the others," said Claudine. "Slip away, Antoinette. Be sure *I* will help *you* if you want me to, since you have done this thing for me."

Some of the fifth formers came up. "What mischief are you thinking of?" said Bobby to Claudine. "You look pleased."

"I was remembering how I said 'I feel as if there will be no sports meeting'," said Claudine. "And I was right, was I not, Bobbee?"

The girls soon forgot about the strange ringing of the fire-bell – all except Mirabel, who felt sure Jane must have done it. In fact, she went even further in her thoughts and suspected Angela of having put Jane up to doing it! She took no notice at all of poor Jane, left her out of the matches, and altogether made her life miserable.

Angela tried to make things up to Jane, delighted at the chance of making a fuss of somebody neglected by Mirabel. Poor Jane was in a great state of mind, upset because Mirabel was unkind to her, thrilled because Angela was sweet to her, and over-tired with all her learning in bed at night with the light of her torch.

She had headaches, felt terribly sleepy all the day, and could not see properly, for she was spoiling her eye-sight by reading in bed by the dim light of the torch.

She was not the only one with headaches just then. Felicity, always more or less afflicted with them, was having them almost continuously. Also, to Anne-Marie's alarm, Felicity had begun to walk in her sleep at night!

This was something that Felicity had done as a child, when her mind was over-taxed, and now she had begun to do it again. Anne-Marie slept in the bed next to Felicity's, and was awakened one night to see a dim white figure stealing out of the door. She sat up and switched on her torch. Felicity's bed was empty!

"Has she gone to the study to do some more work?" thought Anne-Marie. "What an idiot she is! I'd better go and get her. She'll get into an awful row if Miss Cornwallis finds out."

Anne-Marie flung her dressing-gown round her shoulders and went after Felicity. To her surprise Felicity did not go n the direction of their study. Instead she went down the stairs and into the assembly room. She climbed up the platform steps, and stood in the middle of the platform.

"Felicity!" whispered Anne-Marie, astonished. "What are you doing! Felicity!"

Felicity took absolutely no notice at all. She bowed gracefully, took a step backwards and then raised her arms as if she was playing a violin. It was queer to see her in the light of the moon that shone through a nearby window.

Up and down went Felicity's right arm, as the girl played an imaginary tune on an imaginary violin. Her eyes were wide open, fixed and staring. Anne-Marie shivered to see them.

She went up the steps and touched Felicity on the arm. The girl made no response. She went on with her tuneless playing, and then bowed as if she had finished. Anne-Marie took her by the arm. To her surprise Felicity came quite readily with her.

"Are you awake or asleep, Felicity?" said Anne-Marie, fearfully, as they went up the stairs. There was no reply. Felicity was fast asleep, though her eyes were wide open.

Anne-Marie took her safely to her bed and got her in. Felicity cuddled down, shut her eyes and breathed deeply. Anne-Marie got into bed too, but lay awake a long time puzzling over Felicity's sleep-walking.

"It must be because she's a genius," thought the jealous Anne-Marie. "She does queer things, as all geniuses seem to do. Sleep-walking must be a sign of genius, I suppose. I wish I did unusual things too. Then maybe every one would think I was a genius – as I am! Suppose I start a little sleep-walking of my own? If only the girls would wake up and see it, it would be a good way of showing them I'm a genius too. But they all sleep so soundly!"

Still, it was an idea, and Anne-Marie pondered over it a good deal, making up her mind that when a suitable chance came she too would sleep-walk!

Felicity did not remember anything about her sleep-walking the next day and was half-inclined to disbelieve Anne-Marie's account of it. She shrugged her shoulders, and went

Felicity raised her arms as if playing the violin

off to her music-lesson. She could not find interest in anything but her beloved music these days.

Anne-Marie was still trying her best to win back Miss Willcox's smiles – but as the only way she knew was by pestering her to read her poems, she was not very successful. She so badly wanted praise and admiration for her talents, that she did not see that Miss Willcox only had time for those who gave praise and admiration to *her*! Miss Willcox was in many ways a grown-up Anne-Marie, posing and posturing, soaking up adulation and flattery from any one who would give it to her. She had no time for people like Anne-Marie, who also demanded it.

For this reason Alison was very much her favourite. Alison had a real gift for making herself a willing slave to people of Miss Willcox's type. Like Jane for Angela, Alison was pleased to do all kinds of jobs at all kinds of hours, if she could please her idol. Miss Willcox took advantage of this, and kept the devoted Alison quite busy.

"It's a pity," said her cousins. "She's even beginning to dress like Miss Willcox – rather untidy and bitty!"

So she was. She would appear in class with a startling belt round her slim waist, or a scarf round her neck, and had even managed to get some pins rather like Miss Willcox wore in her hair – only Alison's were gilt-topped, not gold!

"Dear little Deirdre fan!" said Bobby, mockingly, when she saw the pins holding back Alison's pretty, curly hair. "Golly, you and Anne-Marie really are a pair! Look at Anne-Marie, she's got on a brooch just like the big ones our Deirdre wears!"

It was really funny to see the way the two girls vied with each other to imitate Miss Willcox. But Miss Cornwallis was not pleased. She eyed the two girls each day, and said nothing at first, for the fifth formers were allowed more freedom with their clothes than the forms below.

But, when Alison appeared with two scarves of different colours twined round her neck, and Anne-Marie came with an out-size pewter brooch that had a brilliant orange stone in the middle, Miss Cornwallis could bear it to longer.

"Have you a sore throat, Alison?" she inquired politely. Alison looked surprised.

"No, Miss Cornwallis," she said.

"Then why *two* scarves, Alison?" said Miss Cornwallis, still in a tone of great politeness, which rang a warning in the ears of the class. How well they knew that extra-polite tone! It always spelt Danger!

"I – I thought they looked nice," stammered Alison, also hearing the warning in that cold, polite voice.

"Well, Alison, I had thought till this term that you had good taste," said Miss Cornwallis. "You always looked tidy and neat and dainty – well-turned out, in fact. But this term you look like a third-rate imitation of some little shop-girl who thinks the more colours and scarves and pins and brooches she wears, the better she looks."

"Oh," said poor Alison, scarlet in the face.

"And Anne-Marie seems to be going the same way," said Miss Cornwallis, looking at the would-be poet in a way that made her squirm and long to take off the enormous brooch. "*What* is that dinner-plate you are wearing, Anne-Marie? Do you think it becomes you?"

Anne-Marie removed the brooch with trembling fingers. She could not bear to have any faults pointed out in public.

"That's better," said Miss Cornwallis. "I don't know if you are imitating any one, either of you – but let me tell you this – imitation is *not* always the sincerest form of flattery when you make yourselves look such silly little sights!"

"Poor little Deirdre fans!" whispered Bobby to Janet. "That was a crack at dear Miss Willcox! I bet Corny knows all about what sillies they are over her!"

That was the end of Alison and Anne-Marie trying to dress like Miss Willcox – but they still went on trying to imitate her deep, drawling voice, her graceful gestures, and her rather round-shouldered walk. The girls got very tired of it, and tried to tease them out of it.

But Alison, thrilled because her dear Deirdre was making such a friend of her, was not in a state to listen to anything

91

the others said, and Anne-Marie was too obstinate. If Alison could imitate Miss Willcox and please her by doing so, then Anne-Marie meant to as well!

Tempers began to be rather short as the exam. drew near. Hard work and worrying about the exam. made most of the fifth form feel harassed and worn. Only Bobby kept cheerful, and Claudine, of course, did not turn a hair. Even Carlotta worried a little, for she wanted to please her father, who had said he would be proud if she passed this rather stiff exam. well.

Pauline worried a lot too. She was not brainless and could do quite well if she tried, but she did not like her study-companion, Alma.

"She's queer," she told Alison. "She doesn't seem to work at all, just sits and stares at her book and eats and eats, like a cow chewing cud. She's always grumbling too – says the food isn't enough here, and she wants more sweets and isn't allowed them. It's awful to swot over your work when a person like that sits opposite, glowering and grumbling and chewing!"

"Poor old Pudding!" said Alison, thinking of the fat, dull Alma, who was always at the bottom of the form. The mistresses did not seem to be unduly upset at Alma's position. In fact, they rather seemed to take it for granted, which was queer. Miss Cornwallis always had a few sharp words to say to any of the others who stayed too long at the bottom of the form! But she rarely spoke sarcastically to Alma about her work.

"It's awful to live with somebody like Alma all the time", sighed poor Pauline. Carlotta heard her and made a suggestion.

"Come in and share our study with me and Claudine when you get too fed up," she said, generously, for she did not really like Pauline very much. "It's a bit bigger than most people's, so there'll be a corner for you if you like. But don't do it too often or you'll get Alma's back up."

"Oh, thank you," said Pauline, gratefully. "It will make such a difference if I can sometimes pop in next door to
92

your study, Carlotta. You will be cheerful company after Alma. She really *is* a pudding!"

Carlotta and Claudine got on very well together. The younger girls who came to do jobs for them liked them very much. Antoinette often came, and strangely enough, never made the kind of extraordinary mistakes she had made in Angela's study!

One day Antoinette found her sister alone and spoke to her with dancing eyes.

"Claudine! Our form is to have a midnight feast! Do you remember telling me of the fine feast you had when you were in the fourth form – you had a midnight picnic by the swimming-pool."

"Yes, I remember," said Claudine, and she sighed. "It is a pity to be in the fifth form. We are so good now. We do not have midnight feasts, we do not play tricks. You will enjoy your feast, my little Antoinette."

"Claudine, could you tell us a good place to keep our cakes and tins and ginger-beer in?" asked Antoinette. "We can't keep them in the common room, and we daren't hide them in our dormitory. Tell me where we can keep them in safety."

Claudine thought hard. "There is a big cupboard just outside my study," she said at last. "It has a key. You shall put your things there, Antoinette, and I will take the key! Then everything will be safe and I can give you the key when you wish for it. You have only to put your head into my study and wink at me – and I will come out with the key!"

"Oh, thank you, a million times!" said Antoinette. "The second form will be so pleased. What a fine sister you are!"

She disappeared, and in due time the cupboard was piled full of eatables and drinks. Claudine removed the key. "Now no one will find them," she said, and hung the key on a nail in her study.

But somebody did find them, which was very unfortunate!

Alma and the Store Cupboard

Alma did not at all like the way Pauline deserted the study they both shared in the evenings. Pauline would sit for a little while, trying to study, then, exasperated by Alma's continually chewing of chocolate, gum or toffee, she would gather up her books and disappear.

"Where are you going?" Alma would call after her. But Pauline did not bother to reply.

So Alma decided to see where Pauline went to. She popped her head out of her study door in time to see Pauline go into the next study, which was Claudine's and Carlotta's. She stood and frowned.

Pauline was not really friendly with either of them – so why, thought Alma, should she keep popping into their study? She sat and brooded over the matter. The next time that Pauline disappeared she made up her mind to follow her into the next study, after a while, and see exactly what she was doing there.

It so happened that Carlotta had had a big box of sugared candies sent to her by her grandmother, and, in her usual generous way, she opened it and laid it on the table in front of Claudine and Pauline.

"Help yourselves whilst you work," she said. Claudine looked longingly at the delicious candied sweets. There were bits of lemon and orange and nut, all candied round beautifully. Claudine, however, thought a great deal of her complexion, which was very good, and she took only one sweet, meaning to make it last all the evening. But Pauline helped herself liberally. She had very little pocket-money to buy herself luxuries, and sweets of this kind did not often come her way.

Just as she was choosing her fourth sweet, the door opened and Alma came in. "Could you lend me a maths book?"

she asked, rather self-consciously. "Oh, *you're* here, Pauline! I say, what gorgeous sweets! You never told me you had a lovely box like that, Pauline."

She thought it was Pauline's box because the girl was helping herself to them. Carlotta gave Pauline no time to reply, nor did Claudine. They both disliked Alma, and were afraid that, seeing Pauline there, she might sit down and stay for the whole evening. Then there would be no sweets left!

"Here's the maths. book, Alma," said Carlotta, and threw her one.

"Shut the door after you," added Claudine.

Alma glared. She thought them very rude, as indeed they were. But who could bear to have Alma sitting there all the evening? Pauline looked uncomfortable as Alma went out and banged the door after her, almost shaking the pictures from the wall.

"She'll be simply beastly to me now,' she said. "I suppose she spied after me and saw where I went. What's the matter with her? She's so terribly fat and pasty-looking."

"Just over-eating, I should think," said Carlotta, beginning to write an essay. "Now shut up for a bit, both of you. I want to think."

Alma was very angry that the three girls in the study had not asked her to have even one sweet. She did no work at all that evening. She sat and brooded over that enormous box of sweets. Alma had a craving for that kind of thing.

"They're mean pigs," she thought. "Really mean. I shall get even with them, though. I'll wait till Carlotta and Claudine are out, and I'll slip in and help myself to a few sweets. I suppose they're Pauline's, and she took them in there to share with the others, instead of sharing them with me."

So Alma kept a watch to see when Carlotta and Claudine went out. There was a little alcove some way up the passage, over which a curtain hung. If she stood there quite quietly she could see when the two girls left their study.

Two evenings later her patience was rewarded. Pauline had gone to a debate. Alma slipped into the alcove and waited to see if Carlotta and Claudine would go to it at half-time, as she had heard them say they would.

Sure enough, in a short while, the study door opened, and Carlotta and Claudine came out. They went down the corridor, talking. Alma waited till their footsteps had died away. She was just going to slip out of the alcove and into the study, when she heard footsteps returning. She peeped out to see who it was.

It was Claudine hurrying back. She had just met Antoinette, who had given her a tin of sugar biscuits to hide in the cupboard with the other things. Claudine ran into her study, took down the key of the cupboard, went outside and unlocked it, pushed in the tin, then locked the door again and hung the key on its nail. Alma watched in the greatest amazement.

Claudine hurried off to join the debate downstairs. Alma stepped out of the alcove, her little eyes gleaming. So that was where the fifth form kept their stores. They must be going to have a party of some kind, and they hadn't told her a word about it! Alma was trembling with rage.

How mean every one was! It had been bad enough in the starchy sixth form the last term, but really, the fifth form were even worse, the way they left her out of things. Alma walked into her own study and sat down heavily. She looked across at the cupboard there. There was absolutely nothing to eat, nothing – and it was ages till supper-time – and even then there wouldn't be much to eat.

She wondered where Claudine kept the key of that store cupboard. It would be fun just to have a peep inside and see what was there – not to *eat* any of it, of course – oh no, thought Alma, she wouldn't do that, mean though the others had been not to ask her to share. But she would dearly like to *look*.

There was no one about at all. She tiptoed to Claudine's

study and pushed open the door. She looked round for the key. Could that be the one, hanging on the nail by the fireplace? She took it off and went to the cupboard in the passage outside.

With trembling fingers she slipped the key into the lock. It turned easily! It *was* the key. Alma opened the cupboard and looked inside.

The things that were there! It seemed as if every single thing she liked was there – sardines and tinned milk, strawberry jam and pineapple in tins, ginger-beer and a box of sweets, biscuits and chocolate.

It was quite impossible for Alma to resist the temptation to pilfer the cupboard. Just one of those chocolates – just a biscuit to go with it – just a sweet or two! Guiltily the girl helped herself, then, hearing footsteps, hurriedly shut the door, turned the key, and slipped back into her own study.

She waited till the footsteps had gone by, then ran into Claudine's study next door, and returned the key to its nail.

For quite a long time Alma sat and brooded over her discovery. She felt certain that the fifth form were going to have a party. She hadn't heard a word about it – but then, nobody ever told her anything!

Alma badly wanted the things in the cupboard. Her continual craving for food made her find excuses for the wrong thing she wanted to do. "It's only right I should share! Even if they don't ask me, I'm a fifth former and I ought to share in their treats. Well, I *shall* share – but in secret, instead of with them at the party! That will punish them for their meanness. It will give them a shock to find a lot of the things gone."

It was a curious secret to have, but Alma found great pleasure in thinking about that store cupboard in bed at night, and in class the next day. She hugged the secret to herself, and gave Claudine many triumphant glances, which the French girl was quite at a loss to understand.

Alma began to go to the store cupboard whenever Claudine's study was empty. She was very artful, for she was

97

careful not to take things whose absence would be very noticeable. She did not take much of the barley sugar in the bottle there, for instance, because she knew it might catch Claudine's eye. But she carefully took all the bottom row of the box of chocolates, which would not be noticed till the first row was eaten. She took a few biscuits from each row in the big tin, not one whole row. She drank half of each ginger-beer bottle, but filled each one up with water so that it would seem as if the bottles had not been tampered with.

She enjoyed being cunning like this. Poor Alma – her whole interest seemed to lie in food, more food and yet more food. Fat, unwieldy and pasty-faced, with no friends, few brains, and a sly, suspicious nature, she was not a happy person.

She had a wonderful time pilfering the store cupboard. Claudine added a few more things to it, never suspecting that many had already gone. Alma was very clever at getting the key, and taking food when no one was about. If she had only used half as much brain in class as she did in stealing from the cupboard, she would not have been so far down at the bottom of the form.

Then one evening something happened. Pauline, Claudine, and Carlotta had gone down to the common room of the fourth form to discuss something with the girls there, and Alma, alone in her study, planned to take some biscuits and some chocolate – perhaps she might even take a tin of sardines, as there were now five or six of them. She could open them when she was alone in her own study.

She stole out and got the key from the study next door. She had just put it into the lock of the cupboard and turned it, when she heard some one coming. In a panic she fled to her own study next door, only just disappearing in time. But the key fell out of the lock with a clang and lay on the floor.

It was Alison coming. She heard the key fall, and was surprised. She picked it up when she came to it, and put it into the cupboard lock. The door swung open – and to Alison's surprise she saw the stores there! She was still staring in amazement when Claudine came along, gave an exclamation and slammed the door shut.

She glared at Alison. "Did you get the key from my study? Well, really, Alison, I did not think it of you! What business is it of yours?"

Alison was puzzled. "From your study?" she said. "Of course not! Some one must have been at the cupboard and opened it when I came along, because I heard footsteps scurrying away, and then heard the key fall out of the lock. I put it back, the door swung open – and I saw the things. I don't want to know anything at all about the food, Claudine, and I certainly shan't tell any one – but it's obvious that somebody knows about the cupboard, isn't it!"

Claudine believed Alison at once. Alison might be weak and silly in many ways, but she was honest and truthful. Claudine swung the door open and looked into the cupboard very thoughtfully. So some one knew of the stores – some one knew where the key was kept – some one knew the secret!

It wasn't long before Claudine discovered that the some-one had also taken various things from the stores. She shut the door and locked it, angry and puzzled.

"Some one's been at the things," she said to Alison, "but as far as I know only I and my little sister Antoinette knew the hiding-place. The second form are to have a midnight feast, and I have kept their food under lock and key for them. Who could have found out the hiding-place – and who could be dishonest enough to steal the things?"

"I can't imagine," said Alison, amazed. "It is such a mean, low-down thing to do. Who ever did it is absolutely despicable. It's unbelievable! Anyway, Claudine, if I were you I'd keep the key somewhere about your person. Then the thief, whoever it is, won't be able to get it!"

Alma heard all this conversation quite clearly, She felt
a wave of anger against Alison. Interfering little busybody!
Now she, Alma, would not be able to feast herself on the
hidden goodies any more. She sat perfectly still, hoping
that neither of the girls would come into her study and see
her there. She felt guilty, and was sure her guilt would show
in her face.

But they did not come. It did not occur to either of them
that the thief would be anywhere near. They felt sure she
had run away. Maybe it was a second former – but how
disgusting, whoever it was!

The next time Alma had a chance of tip-toeing into the
study next to hers, the key was missing. She had feared it
would be. She supposed that Claudine had it round her
neck in safety. Now Alma would not be able to enjoy those
delicious, deceitful little feasts any more!

The girl made a curiously big thing out of the whole
happening, and for a few days thought of nothing else. She
hated Alison for being the unwitting cause of depriving her
of the food she craved for.

"I'll pay her out," she thought. "Spoiling things for
me like this! I'll get even with her."

Alma was strangely clever in underhand ways. Stupid
people can often be cunning, and Alma was no exception.
She set her wits to work, and Alison began to go through
an unpleasant and most annoying time.

Things kept disappearing out of her study. Never
Angela's things, but always Alison's.

"*Where's* my hair-slide?" wailed Alison; "it's gone,
and I only *saw* it on the window-sill this morning. Have
you borrowed it, Angela?"

"Of course not," said Angela. "You've dropped it somewhere."

Then it was Alison's hair-brush that disappeared from her dressing-table in the dormitory. She hunted all over for it, and then had to report the loss to Matron, who was not very pleased.

"How can you possibly mislay a *hair*-brush?" she said to Alison. "I suppose you've been using it in a bedroom battle or something, and it's flown out of the window!"

"We fifth formers don't have bedroom battles," said Alison, with much dignity.

Then her geometry outfit went. It completely and utterly vanished, and no amount of hunting brought it to light. Bobby had two and lent her one.

"But for goodness' sake don't lose it," she said. "You seem to be losing everything this term!"

The same day Alison's knitting needles disappeared out of the scarf she was knitting, and the stitches all pulled out loose when she took the work out of her bag.

"Now this is very queer," said Alison, and she held it up to show Angela. "Look – the needles are gone – and all the stitches are dropped. Angela – what do you think of that?"

"Well," said Angela, "I think some one's doing beastly things to you, Alison. I do really. And I bet I know who it is, too!"

"Who?" said Alison, feeling shocked and hurt.

"Some one who is awfully jealous of you," said Angela.

"You don't mean – Anne-Marie?" said Alison, still more shocked. "Oh *Angela* – surely she wouldn't do mean things like this! Do you think that she's been taking all those things of mine that disappeared too? Oh *no* – she couldn't be as low down as that."

"People say that when any one is jealous they don't mind what they do," said Angela. "And you know Anne-Marie is awfully jealous because you are so well in with your dear Deirdre, and at the moment she isn't in Deirdre's good books. Why she can't see that her dear idol is bored stiff with her poems I really don't know!"

"She's a beast if she is really taking my things, and spoil-

101

ing my knitting," said Alison, almost in tears. The girl always loved to be liked by every one, and it hurt her very much to think that one of her own form could be so unkind. "I shan't listen to a single one of her silly poems now."

So, much to Anne-Marie's surprise, neither Angela nor Alison evinced the slightest interest in a long new poem, called "The Weary Heart", when she went along to their study to read out loud that evening.

"We're busy," said Alison, shortly.

"And you ought to be, too," said Angela, virtuously. "The exam. is coming jolly near."

"It won't take long to read my poem to you," said Anne-Marie, crest-fallen. "This is how it begins . . ."

"Do get out," said Angela. "I'm doing maths. and they don't go with poetry, even if the poem *is* called 'The Weary Heart', which is very descriptive of mine at the moment."

"Why don't you write a poem called 'The Missing Knitting-Needles?'," said Alison, unexpectedly. Anne-Marie stared at her puzzled.

"Why knitting-needles," she inquired at last.

"Well, you ought to know, oughtn't you?" said Alison. But Anne-Marie didn't. Thinking that Alison and Angela were rude and unkind, and a little mad, she went away, carrying her precious poem with her. She bumped into Miss Willcox on her way, and gave a gasp.

"Oh – Miss Willcox – please would you read this? I spent hours over it last night."

Miss Willcox took the poem and glanced at it. It was the same kind as usual, pretentious, full of long words, solemn, sad and far too long. Miss Willcox felt impatient. She determined to be candid with Anne-Marie, now that she had her alone.

"Look here, Anne-Marie," she said, in her deep voice. "I want to give you a little advice – and I want you to listen to it carefully, and follow it."

"Oh *yes*, Miss Willcox," said Anne-Marie, fervently. "I will, indeed I will."

"Well," said Miss Willcox, "you can't write poetry, and you may as well know it. You can rhyme and get the metre right – but your ideas are rubbish. *Real* poetry has ideas in it, beautiful pictures, great feelings. Tear up all your poems, Anne-Marie, and set your mind on the coming exam. That is my advice to you. You think you're a genius. Well, you're not! You are just an ordinary little school-girl who has got a swelled head, and thinks she can write. It is my opinion that unless your character changes considerably, you never *will* write a really good poem!"

Miss Willcox swept off, glad to have relieved her mind of the irritation that Anne-Marie and her never-ending poems always aroused in her. Anne-Marie, struck absolutely dumb, gazed after her, too hurt even for tears.

Her knees felt rather weak. She went to her study and sat down. Felicity was there, conning over some music theory, humming softly to herself. She did not even see Anne-Marie come in.

It took a little time for all that Miss Willcox had said to sink in. Poor Anne-Marie had had the greatest shock of her life. All her great ideas about herself began to totter and waver. *Wasn't* she a genius? *Couldn't* she write marvellously? She began to feel as if she wasn't Anne-Marie any more – she was nobody, nobody at all. She gave a sudden loud sob that entered even Felicity's ears.

"What's up?" said Felicity, looking round.

"Oh, *you* wouldn't understand!" said Anne-Marie, bitterly. "You're a genius, you don't seem to live in this world, you don't notice anything that goes on at all. You don't even know I'm here half the time. Well, what does it matter? I'm nobody, not even Anne-Marie, I've had everything stripped away from me, everything I cared about."

"Don't exaggerate so," said Felicity, mildly surprised at this curious out-burst. "Can't you find the right rhyme for one of your poems? Is that what has upset you?"

"Oh, you're im*poss*ible!" said Anne-Marie, and threw a book at Felicity, which surprised her even more. Anne-

103

Marie went out of the room. Felicity was at once absorbed in her work again, little creases between her eyes, her headache bothering her as usual.

Anne-Marie was hurt, shocked and resentful. She wondered if Miss Willcox could possibly be right. After all, she knew about poetry, so she ought to know if Anne-Marie's was good or bad. Anne-Marie thought a great deal about Miss Willcox that evening, and what she had said.

Her resentment made her begin to see the English mistress rather more clearly than usual. She remembered how the girls laughed at her posing and pretence, her vague ways and soulful looks. Almost in a flash her adoration turned to detestation. Poor Anne-Marie – all the things she cared for had indeed been reft from her suddenly. Her pride in herself and in her genius was gone, her hopes for the future, her confidence that Miss Willcox liked and admired her, even her poems now seemed worthless.

She half thought she would do as Miss Willcox had so coldly advised her, and tear them up. But a doubt still persisted in her mind about the teacher's ability to know, really *know* whether her, Anne-Marie's, poems were good. Suppose she tore them up, and wrote no more – and suppose after all Miss Willcox was wrong, and her poems *were* good – what a loss to the world they might be!

"If only I could find out whether or not Miss Willcox is as good a judge as she always sets out to be!" thought Anne-Marie, quite obsessed by the subject. "But how could I? I don't see *how* I could."

Then a way came to her, and she thought so deeply about it that she didn't even hear Alison speaking to her as she passed. "I'll do it!" thought Anne-Marie, exultantly. "I'll do it! I'll find some little-known poem of one of the very great poets – Matthew Arnold perhaps, or Browning – and I'll write it out in my own hand-writing – and next time we have to write a poem for Miss Willcox, I'll send in, not a poem of my own, but a classic!"

She got up to go to the school library to look through the books of poets there.

"If Miss Willcox praises the poem, I shall know she genuinely appreciates good poetry – if she sneers at it, thinking it is mine, I shall know she doesn't! Ah, Miss Willcox, we shall see!"

Anne-Marie was soon busy turning over the pages of Matthew Arnold, Tennyson, and Browning. She felt as if her whole happiness, her whole future depended on this. She must be careful not to choose a poem at all well-known, or certainly Miss Willcox would recognize it. She must choose one as like her own style as possible – something yearning and soulful and rather high-brow. Ah, Anne-Marie meant to test Miss Willcox, no matter whether she cheated or not in doing so!

Now that her liking for Miss Willcox had so suddenly vanished, Anne-Marie's jealousy of Alison disappeared too. Silly little Alison, she thought, pityingly, as she shut one book of poems and opened another.

But Alison, not knowing anything about Miss Willcox's unkindness to Anne-Marie, and its result, still thought that the other girl was jealous of her, and put down the annoying disappearances of her things to spite on Anne-Marie's part.

Alma knew this and rejoiced. It made things much easier for her, if Alison so clearly suspected some one else! She took a few more things, enjoying poor Alison's exasperation and annoyance. To Alma the loss of the hidden food in the cupboard was as great a blow as Miss Willcox's words had been to Anne-Marie!

Mirabel Is Very High-handed

The second formers decided to have their feast in their own dormitory, which was conveniently far from any mistress's quarters. They asked the first form to join them and there was great rejoicing among the younger ones at this.

"Jolly decent of them," said Sally. "I vote we get in a spot of food ourselves. Don't you think so, Jane?"

Jane was not as thrilled as the others. She had been very quiet and subdued lately, hurt at Mirabel's neglect of her, and at her unjust suspicion regarding the ringing of the fire-bell, which mystery still had not been cleared up. She worked hard for Angela, finding comfort in the older girl's liking and praise, and still did a good deal of her work at night under the sheets.

"Cheer up, Jane!" Sally kept saying. "You look like a hen caught in the rain. *Do* cheer up!"

Jane tried to smile. She had been very afraid of suddenly bursting into tears lately, a most unusual thing for her to do. "It will be fun having a midnight feast," she said, trying to think it *would* be fun. But somehow nothing seemed fun lately. It was so awful to be left out of matches, when she knew she was better than the others. What was the use of practising hard every spare minute she had, when Mirabel kept treating her like this? It wasn't fair, thought Jane, resentfully. It really wasn't.

Claudine had told Antoinette of the pilfering of the cupboard, and the second formers were annoyed and puzzled, for Antoinette had told no one of the hiding-place. Still there was plenty of food left, so never mind!

Antoinette went to Claudine. "Claudine, we are to have our feast tomorrow night. Can I have the key of the cupboard please? I and one of the others will come up here very quietly just before midnight, and get the things."

"Here is the key," said Claudine, taking it off a thin string she wore round her neck. "Now don't make a noise tomorrow night, whatever you do. Have a good time! I wish I was coming too!"

Antoinette grinned. She was enjoying this first term at St. Clare's. Like Claudine, she had slipped out of things she did not like, had played many undetected pranks, and had enjoyed the fun and the jolly companionship. She took the key and went off. She hadn't gone far before she re-traced her footsteps.

How many bottles of ginger-beer were there? Would there be enough, now that the first form was coming? She slipped the key in the lock and turned it.

Alma, in her study, heard the click of the lock. How well she knew it! She peeped out of the door. Why, it was Antoinette at the cupboard, not Claudine. She went out of the door. Antoinette jumped violently and shut the door.

"What have you got in that cupboard?" said Alma, in a smooth voice. "Let me see."

Before Antoinette could object she grabbed the key from her and opened the cupboard. Then she pretended to be very surprised at the contents. "Good gracious! What is all this? Does it belong to you, Antoinette?"

Antoinette hesitated. She disliked Alma and did not trust her. But what could she do? If she was rude, Alma might be most unpleasant.

"I see it is a secret," said Alma, longing to take one of the tins of pine-apple. "Give me one of those tins, Antoinette, and I will not tell any one of this at all. I suppose you are going to have a midnight feast?"

"Yes, tomorrow," said Antoinette, disliking Alma even more. "I'm sorry I can't give you a tin, Alma. I should have to ask the others first. It is not a nice thing for you to ask, anyway – I do not like a bargain of this sort!"

Antoinette shut the door firmly and locked it again, before Alma had made up her mind what to do. She took the key from the lock and stuffed it into her pocket, eyeing Alma defiantly. "I will ask the others if you *may* have a tin of pine-apples, if you wish me to, Alma," she said. "But – surely you do not wish me to?"

Alma scowled. Of course she could not have Antoinette telling the second form that she wanted a tin of pine-apple. She tried to laugh it off.

"Don't be silly! I didn't really mean it. I don't like pine-apple. Well – I hope you enjoy your feast!"

"You won't tell tales of us, will you?" said Antoinette, distrusting Alma more and more. "You promise that, won't you? The second form would think you were terrible to tell such a tale, Alma. You have the English sense of honour, have you not, this honour that always you English girls are talking of?"

"Of course," said Alma, walking off with what dignity she could muster. She went into her study. She thought of the food in that cupboard. She thought of Antoinette's half-veiled insolence. Probably she *would* tell the second formers about the tin of pine-apples she had asked for – and they would nudge each other when she passed, and giggle.

Alma wished she *could* tell tales, and get the feast stopped! But who would listen to her? She would not dare to carry tales to Miss Theobald or Miss Cornwallis, nor was she certain that Hilary, the head-girl of the form, would even listen to her!

Then a thought struck her. What about Mirabel? Mirabel was so keen on sports – and there was a match the day after next! She would not be at all pleased if she knew that the first and second form were going to have a midnight feast just before the match. Mirabel should be told about it, and maybe, in her blunt, overbearing way, she would stop it. That would punish Antoinette all right!

Alma did not dare to go to Mirabel direct. She printed a note, so that her handwriting would not be recognized, and did not sign her name at the end.

"DO NOT EXPECT THE THIRD TEAM TO WIN ITS MATCH ON FRIDAY," said the note. "THEY WILL ALL BE UP AT MIDNIGHT!"

Mirabel found the note on her table in the study that evening. She picked it up in curiosity and read it.

"Gladys!" she said, tossing the note over to her, "what in the world does this mean?"

Gladys read it distastefully. "It's a wretched anonymous letter," she said, "sent by some one who wants to tell tales and doesn't dare to do it openly. Beastly. Tear it up and put it in the waste-paper basket. Don't take any notice of it. That's the way to treat letters of that sort."

"Yes, but Gladys – the third lacrosse team *won't* win their match if they are up at midnight," argued Mirabel.

108

"And I do want them to. I've set my heart on it. I suppose they're going to have a midnight feast or something, silly kids. They'll be tired out next day."

"Well, didn't *you* enjoy midnight feasts when you were in the lower forms?" said Gladys. "Have you forgotten what fun they were?"

"We didn't have them just before an important match," said Mirabel. "We didn't, Gladys."

"For goodness' sake don't think of stopping the feast, or whatever it is," said Gladys, alarmed. "You can't interfere like that, Mirabel, and be such a spoil-sport."

Mirabel thought for a few moments. "I know what to do. I'll send a note to Katie, who's head of the second form, and inform her that I have heard there is to be something going on at midnight tomorrow, and I would like her to see that it is put off till after the match. They will respect my wishes I am sure – then they can play the match properly without being tired, and have their feast afterwards."

"Well, I shouldn't even do that," said Gladys. "I don't think the feast will really make much difference to the match – and anyway, only about a quarter of the girls are playing in it – hardly that!"

"You never back me up in anything now," said Mirabel, frowning. She said no more, but busied herself in writing a short note to the head-girl of the second form.

Katie got it that day and read it in surprise. She showed it into Antoinette. "However did Mirabel get wind of our plans?" she said. "Have you told any one, Antoinette?"

"Well – only Alma," said the French girl, and she told Katie what had happened at the store cupboard.

"How awful!" said Katie, shocked at the tale and at Alma's behaviour. "I say – I wonder if she was the one who pilfered our stores!"

"Perhaps," said Antoinette. "She is not a nice girl, that one."

Katie called a meeting of the second formers in the common room and read them Mirabel's note. It was, as might be expected, rather arrogant and peremptory. Evidently

Mirabel expected to be obeyed, and that was that.

"I vote we have the feast tomorrow night as planned," said Yolande. "Mirabel has been throwing her weight about too much lately. I call that a most uncivil note. Anyway, what business is it of hers? She's always interfering now."

Every one followed Yolande's lead. It was curious how unpopular Mirabel had become. She had tried to drive every one too fast, and now they were digging their toes in and refusing to budge!

"I'd better not answer this note of Mirabel's to-day, had I?" said Katie. "I'll answer it *after* we've had the feast, then she can't stop it!"

Mirabel was surprised to have no answer from Katie, giving an undertaking to postpone the feast till after the match, but it did not occur to her at all that the first and second formers would dare to defy her. She felt puzzled and thought that Katie was not very mannerly – surely she knew that an answer should always be sent at once to any request from one of the top form girls?

The first and second form were getting excited. It was the first time they had had a feast at night, and to them it seemed a terribly exciting thing. Every single girl was going. Violet was back from the san. now after a bout of flu, and was looking forward to it too.

Jane tried to look forward to it, but she was feeling very unhappy. Then a dreadful quarrel blew up between her and Violet, and Jane felt as if she couldn't bear things any more!

Violet had come back from the san. expecting to do Angela's jobs as usual. She had been disappointed because Angela had not even sent a kindly message to her when she was ill. Never mind – Angela would be very glad to see her back, doing her cleaning and mending as before, thought Violet.

But Angela didn't want Violet mooning round again. She had got used to the quiet and efficient little Jane, who, so long as she got a smile and a word of praise now and again, seemed to be quite content. Violet was too talkative, and

110

always liked to recount all her thoughts and doings, which was very boring to the self-centred Angela.

So, to Violet's enormous dismay, Angela did not greet her warmly, and merely informed her that perhaps she would like to go and see to Pauline's jobs, as Jane was doing everything necessary. Violet did not dare to argue with Angela, but rushed off to Jane at once.

"You underhand thing!" she said, her eyes sparkling with anger. "You go behind my back when I'm ill – and worm yourself into Angela's good graces again – and do all the things she was letting me do. Jane Teal, I shall never speak to you again, and neither will half the first form!"

Jane tried to defend herself, but Violet had a ready tongue, and could say some bitter, cutting things. Jane was tired out and unhappy, and she burst into tears.

"Just like you!" said Violet, scornfully. "You think you'll get sympathy just because you cry. Well – you just burst into tears with Angela, and see what *she* says! She can't stand anything of *that* sort!"

Jane could not help feeling that perhaps she *had* done a mean trick to Violet. She hardly slept at all that night, and in the morning she awoke with a sore throat and a head-ache, which made her feel more miserable than ever. "It's a good thing I'm not playing in the match tomorrow!" she thought and wondered if Mirabel would ever put her name down for a match again.

Jane felt rather queer that day. She had a high tempera-ture and didn't know it. She did badly on the lacrosse field and Mirabel ticked her off. She could not concentrate in class and Miss Roberts was not pleased. Violet avoided her and some of the other first formers, who were friends of Violet's, did not speak to her either.

"I wish I was at home," thought Jane, longingly. "If I could just tell Mother all about it I'd feel better. I can't write it in a letter. I wish I could go home."

The idea grew and grew in her worried mind and at last Jane made a plan she would never have made if she had been quite well. Instead of going to the feast she would go home! Luckily for her, her home was actually in the next village, four miles away. Jane felt sure she could easily walk there in the middle of the night! Then she would see her mother, tell her everything, and things would be all right again.

She did not know she was beginning to have flu and had a temperature, she had no idea she was not normal just then. Sally could not get a word out of her and was worried. Poor Jane – she was not having an easy time just then. But never mind, she thought, I'll be home tonight!

A Surprising Night

That Friday night was to be a most astonishing one for Mam'zelle, though she did not know it. She never forgot it, and, whenever she took a holiday in her beloved France, she would often recount the happenings of that night, to show her enraptured listeners how queer were the English girls!

It was the night of the Feast, and the first and second formers were to have it at twelve o'clock sharp in one of their dormitories. Antoinette had already secreted some of the things on the top of a high cupboard in her dormitory, and meant to fetch the rest just before midnight.

Mirabel, unfortunately, had seen Antoinette hurrying along the corridor outside her study, carrying various suspicious parcels. She had called after Antoinette, but Antoinette had thought it advisable not to hear, and had scurried fast round the corner, almost knocking over Miss Willcox.

Mirabel stared after the disappearing Antoinette in exasperation. Really, these kids were getting too uncivil for words. She went back into her own study and frowned. *Could* those kids be going to have their feast that night after all – when she had asked them not to? Could they flout her request in that way – surely not!

All the same a doubt persisted in Mirabel's mind, and she could not get rid of it. She said nothing to Gladys, but she made up her mind to keep awake that night, and to go along to the first or second form dormitories about midnight, to see if anything was happening.

"And if there is – won't I give them a talking to!" thought Mirabel, grimly. "I'll report them too. I'll make them see they can't disregard *my* orders!"

Now Anne-Marie had planned to stage a sleep-walking act that night. She had thought of quite a lot of things to do which were extraordinary, and might make people say "Ah, she does those because she's a genius," as so often was said of the absent-minded Felicity. But she rather doubted her ability to carry them off in front of the sharp-eyed, quick-minded members of the fifth form.

It would never do to put on some sort of genius act, and have the others roar with laughter, disbelieve in it, and tell her it was all put on. It was getting to be quite imperative to Anne-Marie to be thought really clever. She had to do something to cancel out the damping effect of Miss Willcox's words.

Who would be taken in most easily? She thought for a while, and then decided on Mam'zelle. She had heard of the many tricks the girls had played on the French Mistress through the years, and she felt sure she would take in Mam'zelle. Mam'zelle would exclaim, and waggle her hands, and tell every one. She would say "Ah, *la petite* Anne-Marie, she walks in her sleep, she recites poetry as she walks, she is a genius! We must be careful of her, we must cherish this talented girl! One day she will be famous!"

Yes, certainly Mam'zelle would be the best one to impress. The middle of the night would be the best time. She would find some means of waking Mam'zelle, and bring her out in the passage, and then she would let her see her,

113

apparently walking in her sleep, reciting lines and lines of poetry. Mam'zelle would be most impressed, and perhaps even Miss Theobald would think that Anne-Marie was a genius, and ask to see some of her poems.

Anne-Marie was really very pleased with her idea. She quite looked forward to putting it into practice that night. "About half-past twelve or so," she thought. "That would be the best time. Every one will be asleep by then."

She had, of course, chosen a most unfortunate night for her sleep-walking, for quite a number of people were going to be wide-awake! All the first and second formers would be revelling in their feast. Jane Teal would be stealing through the school, meaning to run off home. Mirabel would be on the prowl to find out if the younger girls were really having their feast. Alma would be snooping about to see if there was likely to be any food left in the cupboard. Antoinette and one or two others would be fetching the rest of the food.

And Felicity was to choose that night for sleep-walking too – but genuine sleep-walking, in her case. So there would be quite a number of people wandering about, though Anne-Marie hadn't the remotest idea of this.

All the girls went off to bed as usual at their ordinary times. The first and second formers went first, giggling with excitement, vowing that they wouldn't sleep a wink till midnight. Antoinette and Sally were to be responsible for rousing any one who *did* go to sleep. It was thrilling to look forward to such an escapade.

The third and fourth formers went off to bed later.

The fifth and sixth could stay up till ten o'clock, and usually did. They all retired as usual, even Felicity, who often did not go till much later, lost as usual in her music. It was astonishing that no mistress had discovered her light burning so late in her study, but so far no one had.

Then the mistresses went to bed, yawning, having a last word together before they parted. Mam'zelle was the last to go. She had a pile of French essays from the sixth form to go through, and had left them rather late.

114

"I will correct these, and then go," she thought, glancing at the clock. "Half-past eleven already! How slow I have been tonight!"

At just about five minutes to twelve Mam'zelle went into her bedroom. At twelve o'clock she was getting into bed, and the bed was about to creak under her rather heavy weight, when some sound caught her ears.

It sounded as if something hard had been dropped on the floor immediately above her head. Mam'zelle sat on the side of the bed and pondered over the various possible causes of the noise.

It was not the cat. It was not the unexpected groan or creak that furniture sometimes gave at night. It was not any mistress on the prowl, because all had gone to bed. Then what could it be? Mam'zelle thought hard. She knew that the fifth form studies were above her bedroom, stretching in a long couple of rows down and around two corridors. Surely no one could possibly be up still? The fifth form must all be in bed!

Another small sound decided Mam'zelle. She had better go and investigate. It might be a burglar. Mam'zelle had a horror of burlgars, but she felt it her duty to find out whether there was one in the school or not. Feeling extremely brave, and arming herself with a hairbrush, she put on her dressing-gown and slippers, tied the girdle tightly round her plump waist, and opened her bedroom door.

All the passages and corridors of St. Clare's were lighted throughout the night, but with specially dimmed lights. It was possible to see a figure, but not to make out who it was. The corridors looked rather eerie to Mam'zelle as she set out on her journey of investigation.

The first thing that Mam'zelle did was to fall over the school cat, who was an enormous black fellow, much given to wandering around at night. Seeing Mam'zelle perfectly clearly, though she could not see him at all, he advanced upon her, and tried to rub against her ankles, delighted to see a fellow-wanderer in the night.

Mam'zelle gave a muffled shriek, and almost overbalanced. One of her big feet caught the cat on its side, and it gave one of its yowls. Mam'zelle recognized the cat's voice, and was relieved to find that it was not a burglar lying on the floor to catch her foot, but only the cat.

"Sssst!" she said, in a piercing, sibilant whisper, and the cat fled, grieved at Mam'zelle's lack of friendliness.

Mam'zelle went up the stairs to the next floor, where she had heard the noise. Antoinette was up there, on her third journey to collect the eatables with Sally. To her horror she suddenly heard Mam'zelle's piercing "Sssst!" noise from the floor below. She clutched Sally.

"Somebody's about! Did you hear that? Oh, how tiresome, Sally! What shall we do?"

"There's an alcove near here," whispered Sally. "Look — where that curtain is. We'll get behind there with our tins and bottles. Quick! Maybe whoever it is will pass by. Don't sneeze or anything!"

The two girls pressed themselves behind the curtain, their hearts beating fast. They heard Mam'zelle's footsteps coming along, making a soft swishing noise in her big bedroom slippers. They stood quite still.

Mam'zelle came to the alcove. She thought the curtain bulged suspiciously, and she put out a trembling hand. She distinctly felt some soft body behind it! She gave a gasp. Antoinette and Sally decided to make a bolt for it, and suddenly shot out from the alcove, dropping a ginger-beer bottle on poor Mam'zelle's toes. She gave an anguished groan, lifted her foot, and did a few heavy hops over to the opposite wall, putting out a hand to steady herself when she got there.

She caught sight of two figures racing down the dim passage, and round the corner. She had no idea whether they were burglars or girls. As she felt her corns tenderly, wrath swept over her. How dared people drop things on her feet in the middle of the night, and the run away without apologizing? Mam'zelle determined to chase the scamps, whoever they were, and run them to earth.

116

She did not see the ginger-beer bottle lying at her feet, and she fell over it as she went swiftly down the passage, stubbing her other foot this time. The bottle went rolling off and hit the wall. Mam'zelle stopped again and groaned.

She ran down the passage and came to the corner. There was no one to be seen there. The passage went completely round the third floor of the building, and came back again where it began, and Mam'zelle thought it would be a good idea to go the whole way and see if any one was about on that floor. So off she set, determined to run to earth who-ever was up so late at night.

Pad-pad-pad, went her feet, and every now and again Mam'zelle set her pince-nez firmly on her nose, for they had an irritating way of jumping off when she ran. Pad-pad-pad – the chase was on!

Mam'zelle on the War-path

Alma was the next one to be dimly seen by Mam'zelle. She had been certain that Antoinette would go to the store cupboard that night, and would probably make two or three visits. Probably in between she would leave the door open. Then, thought greedy Alma, she might be able to pop in and take something for herself. A tin of pine-apple for instance. She seemed to crave for a tin of pine-apple!

So, making sure that the rest of her dormitory were asleep, Alma rose quietly from her bed, and went up the stairs to the third floor. She made her way to the cupboard just at the same moment as Mam'zelle, panting, came round the last of the four corners of the corridor, back again to where the alcove was. The store cupboard was quite near.

Mam'zelle saw a figure in the passage. Ah – there was *one* of the midnight wanderers, at least! Mam'zelle would teach them to drop things on her poor toes! She crept up behind the unsuspecting Alma, who was half in the cup-board, groping about for a tin of some kind.

117

Alma had the shock of her life when she felt a hand on her shoulder. She lunged out in fright and struck poor Mam'zelle square in the middle. Mam'zelle doubled up at once, and gave such a deep groan that Alma was horrified. She could not move an inch, but stood there, trembling.

Mam'zelle recovered rapidly. She felt certain that this must be a burglar rifling cupboards. He was dangerous! He had given her a terrible blow, the big coward! Mam'zelle was not going to come to grips with him. Giving Alma a sudden push, which landed her among the tins, bottles and old rugs, she shut the door firmly, locked it, and took the key.

"Ha!" said Mam'zelle, addressing the alarmed Alma in the cupboard. "Now I have you under key and lock! I got for the police!"

With this terrifying threat she padded off to telephone to the police. She went downstairs, congratulating herself heartily on her smartness and bravery, and feeling her middle tenderly to see if she was bruised.

As soon as she got downstairs she saw Jane Teal, who had chosen that moment to creep away from the others, put on her hat and coat and go to find a side-door she could open quietly. But poor little Jane was now feeling very ill. The flu was sending her temperature high, and she felt as if she was in a dream. All she wanted was to get to her mother, and to do that she knew she must get out of St. Clare's and walk and walk.

So, hardly knowing what she was doing, she felt with a feverish hand along the wall to find the side-door. She muttered to herself as she went. "I must find the door. That's the first thing. I must find the door."

Mam'zelle heard the muttering and stopped in amazement and alarm. Could this be yet another burglar? Who was this person groping along the wall – with a hat on too! Mam'zelle could not see in the dim light what kind of person it was, but having got the idea of burglars firmly in her mind, she felt certain this must be another – probably the second of the two she had first seen racing down the upstairs

118

passage. She began to tiptoe cautiously after Jane.

Jane felt along the wall till she came to a door. "Here is a door," she muttered. "I must open it and go out. I've found a door."

But it was not the side-door, leading into the garden. It was the door of the second form games cupboard, full of lacrosse sticks, old goal-nets, a few discarded rain-coats and such things as these. Jane opened the door and went into the cupboard. Mam'zelle, triumphant, saw a chance of repeating her recent brilliance, and of locking this second burglar into a cupboard too.

She darted forward, shut the door and locked it, leaving poor Jane in the darkness among things that felt most extraordinary to her hot little fingers.

"I want to go home," said Jane and suddenly sank down on to a pile of sticks and nets, for her legs felt as if they would no longer carry her. She lay there, feverish and half-dreaming, not knowing or caring in the least where she was.

Mam'zelle could not help feeling very proud of herself. What other mistress at St. Clare could catch and imprison two burglars in one night like this? Mam'zelle began to think she was wasted as a French mistress. She should have been in the police force.

"Now I got to the telephone," she said to herself, thinking with delight of the astonishment of the police when they heard her news. But she was not yet to broadcast her news, for, even as she went into the hall, she saw somebody else!

This time it was Felicity, walking in her sleep, trying to find the assembly room, so that she might once again mount the platform, and play her imaginary violin. She walked solemnly, her eyes wide open, humming a melody in a low, soft voice. She had on her white night-gown, and Mam'-zelle was absolutely petrified to see this figure, walking towards her, making a queer low humming.

"*Tiens!*" said Mam'zelle, and took a step backwards. For the first time she began to wonder whether the night's happenings were real or whether she might be dreaming. It seemed astonishing that so many people were about, in the middle of the night.

This could not be a burglar. It looked like something unearthly – a spirit wandering about, lost and lone! Mam'zelle shivered. Burglars she had been able to deal with – but spirits were different. They faded away, they disappeared into thin air, if they were touched, and Mam'zelle did not like things of that sort.

She decided not to go to the telephone just then, as she would have to meet this wandering spirit face to face. She would retire to her bedroom for a little while till the spirit had returned to wherever it had come from. So Mam'zelle turned tail and fled.

But for some reason Felicity, fast asleep as she was, seemed to perceive Mam'zelle as she disappeared towards the stairs. Into her dreaming mind came the idea that this person might take her to the platform, so that she might play her wonderful composition, and she followed Mam'zelle up the stairs, her eyes glassy and wide open, her hands outstretched.

Mam'zelle glanced behind and was most alarmed to find the white spirit following her. She had not bargained for this at all. She almost ran to get to her bedroom on the second floor.

Felicity followed, seeming almost to float up the stairs, for she was tall and thin, and much too light for her age. Mam'zelle bolted into her bedroom and sat down on her bed, out of breath.

The door opened and Felicity came in, her eyes still wide open. As Mam'zelle had her light on, she saw at once that what she had thought was a frightening apparition was only Felicity.

"*Tiens!*" said Mam'zelle, putting her hand up to her forehead. "*Tiens!* What kind of a night is this, when burglars and children walk around. Felicity, my child, are you awake?"

There was something rather terrifying about Felicity's white, unawakened face. Mam'zelle saw that she was sound asleep, and was afraid to wake her. She was more than relieved when Felicity, feeling her bed, drew back the covers, got into it and shut her eyes. In a minute or two she was apparently sleeping quite peacefully.

Mam'zelle stared down at the pale face on her pillow. To have two burglars shut into two separate cupboards and a sleep-walking girl in her bed was rather bewildering. She could not make up her mind whether to telephone to the police or to go and call Miss Theobald and show her Felicity. Mam'zelle had had enough experience of girls to know that sleep-walking was not a good thing – something had happened to make Felicity act in this way, and that something must be investigated.

There was a noise upstairs again. Antoinette and Sally had returned to the cupboard for eatables, and had found the door locked, the key gone, and a prisoner in the cupboard! In amazement and fear they fled back to their dormitory to tell the others. Mam'zelle, disturbed by the noise they made, went out of her bedroom, and, as an afterthought, turned the key in the lock, in case Felicity should try a little more sleep-walking.

She was just in time to see Antoinette and Sally, two vague figures in the distance, running back to their dormitory.

"*Tiens!*" said Mam'zelle again, thunderstruck to find yet more people abroad that night. "Do I sleep or wake? Everywhere I go I see people fleeing in the night!"

The next person Mam'zelle saw was Mirabel, who was creeping down the stairs to see if the second formers were holding their feast after all. Mam'zelle could not believe her eyes. Was the whole school wandering about that night – or was this yet another burglar?

Mirabel was a tall, strapping girl, and she wore pyjamas. In the dim passage she looked as big as a man, and Mam'zelle felt certain this must be another of the gang of burglars that appeared to be infesting St. Clare's that night. She followed her, trying to make no noise at all. It was becoming quite a common-place for Mam'zelle to lock people up

121

that night, and she fondly imagined she could somehow imprison this burglar also.

Mirabel went towards the second form dormitories. Mam'zelle, afraid that the burglar might scare the girls there, hurried her steps. The school cat reappeared at this moment, and tripped poor Mam'zelle up, so that she made a noise. Mirabel looked round, and slipped quickly into one of the bathrooms that ran opposite the dormitories. She did not want any of the second formers to know she was snooping round, in case by any chance they were *not* holding the feast after all.

Mam'zelle saw with great pleasure that once again she could lock somebody into somewhere. She began to think that burglar-catching was the easiest thing in the world – merely a matter of turning a key in a lock. She turned the key in the shut bathroom door – and there was yet another burglar accounted for!

Mam'zelle thought with delight of the surprise and admiration of the other mistresses when they heard of her exploits. She felt ready to imprison half a dozen more burglars into cupboards if necessary.

Mirabel was horrified at being locked in. She had no idea who had turned the key, but thought it was some silly trick of one of the younger girls. So she settled down to wait for the door to be undone. She felt sure no girl would keep her imprisoned all night long.

Mam'zelle decided that she would now go to Miss Theobald, as she felt that no policeman would be inclined to believe a telephone call from her about three locked-up burglars. So she padded along the passage to the stairs – but just as she was about to descend them, she caught sight of yet another night wanderer.

This time it was Anne-Marie, who was now putting on her sleep-walking act in imitation of Felicity, and was on her way to wake up Mam'zelle. Mam'zelle could not believe her eyes when she saw yet another sleep-walker. No, really she must be going mad! There could not be so many people rushing about at night in the school passage!

Anne-Marie saw Mam'zelle standing under one of the dimmed lamps, and recognized her. At first she got a shock, for she had expected Mam'zelle to be in bed and not ambling about. But as soon as she was sure it really *was* Mam'zelle, she acted exactly as if she was walking in her sleep. She glided by Mam'zelle, her eyes set and staring just as Felicity's had been, muttering a poem.

Mam'zelle hesitated to grab her, for she had heard it was bad to awaken sleep-walkers suddenly. So she did not touch Anne-Marie, but followed her, whispering under her breath.

"The poor child! Here is another who walks in her sleep! I will follow her."

Anne-Marie led Mam'zelle a fine dance, and finally ended up outside the second form dormitories. The girl on guard there gave the alarm when she saw the two figures coming, and there was a terrific scramble as bottles and tins and plates were pushed under beds. The candles were blown out and girls got hurriedly into bed, those who didn't belong to that dormitory squeezing into wardrobes and under beds.

Anne-Marie, still acting, wandered into the second form dormitory, meaning to walk to the end and back – but she fell over an empty bottle, and gave an exclamation. Mam'-zelle followed her into the room and switched on the light.

Anne-Marie, dazed by the sudden light, blinked in confusion, watched in amazement by girls in bed. Then, re-membering her sleep-walking act, she once again became glassy-eyed and glided between the beds.

The girls sat up, giggling. "She's pretending!" called Antoinette.

"Ah, no, she walks in her sleep, the poor, poor child," said Mam'zelle. "What can we do for her?"

"I will cure her, *ma tante*," said the irrepressible Antoinette, and leapt out of bed. She took a jug of cold water and threw it all over poor Anne-Marie, who, angry and wet, turned and gave Antoinette such a ticking off that all the girls knew at once that she certainly had not been sleep-walking before, but only play-acting. Mam'zelle realized it

123

Antoinette threw the jug of cold water at Anne-Marie

too, and tried to haul Anne-Marie out of the room, scolding her vigoriously, and telling her to go and change her wet things at once. So engrossed was she that she entirely failed to see any signs of the midnight feast, nor did she notice any of the girls squashed into the wardrobes or under the beds.

"Golly!" said Sally, as soon as Mam'zelle had gone off with Anne-Marie. "I don't believe she even *saw* the signs of our feast, not even that bottle that rolled out from under a bed!"

"Bit of luck for us," said Violet. "Come on, let's finish everything up quickly, and hide the things and get to bed before Mam'zelle thinks of coming back!"

The girls giggled. Mirabel, shut in the bathroom just opposite heard them, and knew they were still enjoying their feast. She grew very angry indeed. She felt certain one of the second formers had locked her in, and she was determined to report the whole lot of them and have them well punished.

Mam'zelle took Anne-Marie to Matron's room, and woke Matron up, explaining volubly about Anne-Marie and why she was wet. Anne-Marie, her sleep-walking act quite ruined, wept copiously, fearing that she would be the laughing stock of the school next day.

"Now stop that silly crying," said Matron, briskly giving Anne-Marie a vigorous rub-down with a very rough towel. She had long ago sized up Anne-Marie as a silly, swollen-headed girl, just the kind to act like this.

"I must go," said Mam'zelle, remembering the various people she had locked up that night. "I have burglars to see to."

Matron stared. "What did you say?" she inquired.

"I said, I have burglars to see to," said Mam'zelle, with dignity. "I have spent the night chasing people round the corridors, and locking them up. I go to Miss Theobald now, and she will telephone to the police. Ah, the people I have chased tonight. You would not believe it, Matron!"

Matron didn't. She thought Mam'zelle must be dreaming. "Well, you go and get Miss Theobald and the police and whatever else you like," she said, rubbing Anne-Marie so hard that she groaned. "But don't bring me any more wet girls to dry in the middle of the night. I don't approve of them."

Mam'zelle went off. She came to Miss Theobald's bedroom and knocked on the door. A surprised voice came from inside.

"Yes? Who is it?"

"It is I, Mam'zelle," said Mam'zelle, and opened the door. "Pardon me for coming at this time of the night, Miss Theobald – but I have burglars locked up in cupboards and a sleep-walker in my bedroom."

A Little Unlocking

Miss Theobald listened to Mam'zelle's tale in the utmost astonishment. It seemed to her as if all the corridors of St. Clare's must have been peopled with burglars, robbers, thieves, and others the whole of the night – but what was even more astonishing was the thought of Mam'zelle, who was terrified even of mice and beetles, valiantly chasing the burglars and, more remarkable still, locking them up wholesale!

She could hardly believe it. She looked closely at Mam'zelle, and wondered if the French mistress could possibly have dreamt it all. She got out of bed and put on her dressing-gown.

"I think, before I telephone the police, you had better show me where you locked these men up," she said.

Mam'zelle trotted her off to the cupboard where she had locked in little Jane Teal. There was no sound from there at all. Miss Theobald was puzzled. She rapped on the door. Still no sound. Jane had fallen into a feverish doze. Miss

Theobald suddenly heard the sound of overloud breathing, quick and hoarse.

She felt sure it was no burglar there. She unlocked the door, to Mam'zelle's dismay, and switched on the light inside the big cupboard – and there, before poor Mam'zelle's startled eyes, lay little Jane Teal, obviously ill, fully-dressed, even to her hat.

"This child's ill," said the Head Mistress, feeling Jane's burning hot hand. "'Flu, I should think, and a very high temperature with it. What on earth is she doing dressed up like this, with hat and coat on? Was she going out?"

Mam'zelle was dumbfounded. She could not think of a word to say. Miss Theobald gently awoke Jane, and helped her to her feet. She could hardly stand. Between them the two mistresses took her to Matron's room, who, at once glance saw that Jane was seriously ill.

"I'll carry her to the san.," she said. "I'll sleep there with her myself tonight."

Matron's capable, strong arms lifted the half-unconscious Jane easily, and bore her away to the quiet and comfortable san. where all the ill girls were nursed. There was no one there at the moment. Matron soon had Jane undressed and in bed with a hot water bottle.

"Well," said Miss Theobald, thankful to have found poor Jane before worse befell her, "what about your next burglar, Mam'zelle?"

Mam'zelle fervently hoped that the next prisoner *would* prove to be a burglar, even if he leapt out at them and escaped! She led the way to the bathroom opposite the second form dormitory.

The second formers were still awake and heard the footsteps and voices in wonder. As the footsteps passed their door, they sat up and whispered. "Who is it? What's up?"

Antoinette leapt out of bed and padded to the door. She peeped out cautiously. To her enormous astonishment she saw the Head Mistress standing by the bathroom door, with Mam'zelle, her aunt! Antoinette gaped as she saw Miss

127

Theobald rap quietly on the door and say, "Who's in here?"

A voice answered something, an angry voice. Miss Theobald heard that it was a girl's voice and not a man's, and she unlocked the door. Out shot Mirabel, expecting to see a group of grinning second formers – and stopped short in amazement when she saw Mam'zelle and the Head Mistress.

Mam'zelle's eyes almost dropped out of her head. She had shut her biggest burglar – or so she thought – into the bathroom – and now it was only Mirabel, that big detestable, loud-voiced Mirabel, whose talk was all of games, games, and yet more games. Mam'zelle snorted in disgust.

"I want to complain," said Mirabel, in a loud voice, surprised but unabashed by the sight of the Head. "I came to see if the second formers were having a midnight feast, which I had forbidden – and one of them locked me in this beastly cold bathroom. I want to report them, Miss Theobald. I know they held a feast, and there's a most important match tomorrow. And I demand that the girl who locked me in shall be punished."

"It was Mam'zelle who locked you in," said Miss Theobald. "You had no right to be wandering about at night like this. Mam'zelle thought you were a burglar and locked you in."

Antoinette stifled a giggle and rushed back into the dormitory. She related in whispers what she had heard. The girls were half-amused and half-angry – amused to think that Mirabel had been locked up, and angry to think she had been sneaking round, and had reported them.

Then Mam'zelle's loud voice penetrated into the listening dormitory. "What is this untruthful thing you say, Mirabel? The second formers had *no* feast tonight! Did not I go there to chase Anne-Marie, after I had locked you in, and the good girls were all in bed and asleep! Not a thing to be seen, not a tin, not a bottle! You are a bad untruthful girl, trying to get others into trouble to protect yourself from blame!"

Mirabel was speechless. She glared at Mam'zelle, and Miss Theobald hastened to intervene.

"Well, if Mam'zelle was in the second form dormitory, and the girls were in bed and asleep, it seems to me that you must be mistaken, Mirabel."

"I'm not," said Mirabel, rudely. "Mam'zelle isn't speaking the truth. Go into the second form dormitory and ask the girls if I or Mam'zelle are right, Miss Theobald. Then you will see."

"I shall do nothing of the sort," said the Head Mistress, coldly. "Be more polite, Mirabel. You forget yourself."

Mirabel, simmering with rage, dared say no more. "Go back to bed," said Miss Theobald. "I will settle this to-morrow. I do not feel very pleased with you, Mirabel."

Mirabel went back to bed with an angry heart. She knew she was right. Those second formers *had* had a feast, and Mam'zelle must be shielding them – because of Antoinette, she supposed. Well, she would get even with the little beasts. She would cancel the match next day! No one should play. She would show those youngsters she was sports captain, and make them toe the line!

"Well," said Miss Theobald, looking at Mam'zelle, as Mirabel retreated, "what about your next burglar, Mam'zelle?"

Mam'zelle took the Head up to the corridor that ran round the fifth form studies. She was feeling rather nervous now that her burglars were all turning into girls. It was really most extraordinary.

Miss Theobald rapped on the cupboard in which Alma was imprisoned. Alma's voice was heard.

"Let me out! It's awful in here!"

The Head unlocked the door, and Alma staggered out, stiff and cold. Miss Theobald looked at her in surprise. "Why were you wandering about at night?" she said, sharply.

"I – er – I heard a noise," said Alma, stammeringly, for she was afraid of the Head. "And some one locked me in that cupboard."

Miss Theobald switched her torch on and lighted up the inside of the cupboard. She saw at a glance that it had been used as a storing-place for food.

"You went to take food from here, I suppose, Alma?" she said. "Was it your own food?"

"I wasn't taking any," said Alma. "I was – well, I was just *looking*."

"This girl is always eating," said Mam'zelle in disgust. "Always she chews something, always she sucks."

"Go back to bed, Alma," said Miss Theobald. "I will see you in the morning."

Alma scuttled off thankfully. Miss Theobald turned rather coldly to Mam'zelle. "Any more burglars?" she asked.

"Oh, Miss Theobald, truly I am sorry to have made so many mistakes!" said Mam'zelle, passing her hand through her hair in bewilderment. "I pray you to forgive me, to . . ."

"Don't worry about it," said Miss Theobald. "It is perhaps a good thing that all this has happened. It seems that a great deal is going on this term at St. Clare's that I must inquire into. Now – who is this girl you had in your bedroom – the one you found sleep-walking?"

"Felicity," said Mam'zelle, fervently hoping that Felicity would still be there. She hurried down the stairs to her room, and unlocked the door.

Felicity was still there, lying asleep in bed. She looked very young and thin and, even in her sleep, her face wore a harassed, worried look. Miss Theobald looked at her for some time.

"This girl is obviously over-working," she said, and sighed. "Her music is too much for her, but her parents insisted on her taking her exams. I think, Mam'zelle, if you don't mind, we'll leave her in your bed. You had better sleep in the bed in Miss Harry's room – she is away for a few days. I suppose you have no more locked-up girls to show me tonight?"

"No," said Mam'zelle, looking so crestfallen that the Head smiled. She patted Mam'zelle's plump arm.

"You meant well," she said. "If they had all been burglars, as you thought, you would have done a good night's work. Anyway, it is a good thing that so many things have come to light. Good night."

Miss Theobald went back to bed, worrying about little Jane Teal, Alma, Mirabel and Felicity. It looked as if Jane had been trying to run away. She must find out about that.

Mam'zelle got into a strange bed, cold and puzzled. Why had so many girls been wandering about that night? Ah, that detestable Mirabel, how dare she say that she, Mam'zelle, was telling an untruth that night? And that dreadful Alma? Did she go snooping round every night to steal food from cupboards? There was something wrong with her, that girl!

"Tomorrow I will talk with Claudine and Antoinette," thought Mam'zelle, screwing up her eyes, trying to go to sleep. "They have good sense, they will tell me everything. It is a pity that English girls have not the good sense of French girls. It will be a pleasure to talk to my good little Claudine and Antoinette – *they* do not wander round at for me to lock up. Alas, to think that I made so many prisoners, and now not one remains!"

A Few Upsets

The next day the whole school knew the story of the night escapades, and how Mam'zelle had locked up so many girls. There was a great deal of giggling and chattering, and Anne-Marie had her leg pulled about her sleep-walking.

"How can I help sleep-walking?" she asked, trying to assume a dignity she did not feel. "Felicity sleep-walks too, doesn't she? And you don't laugh at *her*."

Miss Willcox heard about Anne-Marie's sleep-walking act and laughed too. She even teased her about it in class, which hurt Anne-Marie more than anything, and made her quite determined to get even with Miss Willcox if she could.

Felicity did not appear in class that day. It was reported that she had gone to the san. for a rest and would not be taking the exam. which was the next week. Jane Teal was very ill indeed. Sally had been allowed to see her and had come back rather scared.

"Matron's worried about her and so is the doctor," said Sally. "Her mother is there in the san., too. I'm not allowed in any more. Matron shooed me out. I heard Matron say that Jane's worried about something and she can't get out of her what it is. But *I* know! It's all this business with Mirabel and Angela, and I know Jane reads in bed late at night with a torch. She learns her English and Latin that way. She told me so."

"Well – hadn't you better go and tell Matron what you know," said Katie. "She might put things right for Jane then."

"She can't, silly," said Sally. "You know what worries Jane more than anything – she's upset because Mirabel believes she rang that fire-bell to stop her meeting, and that's why Mirabel is so beastly to her. If only we could find out who did ring that bell, and make them own up, it would take a great load off poor Jane's mind!"

Violet Hill was feeling uncomfortable that morning, when she heard how ill Jane was. She remembered her quarrel with Jane, and the unkind things she had said. She wished she hadn't now.

"It will be a good thing to play in the match this afternoon," said Sally. "Take our minds off everything! We'll feel better out on the field, playing or watching."

But Mirabel threw a bomb-shell that morning. She put a notice on the board, and soon every one was round it astonished and angry.

"The match today is cancelled, owing to the behaviour of the team members," said the notice, and it was signed by Mirabel.

"*Well!*" said Sally. "Would you believe it! How has she got the nerve to stick up a notice like that? And what right has she to cancel our match?"

"She's got the right because she's sports captain," said Violet. "Beast! I vote we send her to Coventry and don't speak a word to her, or smile at her, or turn up at any practices at all!"

Every one agreed. It was an unheard of thing for the lower forms to treat an upper form girl in this way, but they felt so indignant that not one member of the first or second form backed out of the agreement. Just because they had dared to have a feast in spite of Mirabel, she was treating them abominably, and putting up a notice in public to make them look small!

Gladys saw the notice and was shocked. She went straight to Mirabel.

"Mirabel! How *could* you put up that notice? Whatever were you thinking of? You *can't* cancel the match!"

"I can and I have," said Mirabel grimly. "I've sent a telegram to the school we were playing. They won't be coming. We shall have a practice match, instead. I have just written out another notice about that – the practice is to be at three o'clock, and every girl must attend from the two lowest forms."

"Mirabel, you must be mad," said Gladys, quite alarmed at her friend's grim face. "You can't put all the girls against you like this, you really can't. You'll only get the worst out of them instead of the best."

"I've told you before that I won't have you interfering with my decisions," said Mirabel.

"Then what is the use of my being vice-captain?" said Gladys. "Not a bit of use! I can't help you, because you won't let me!"

"Well, you're not much use, if you really want to know," said Mirabel, coldly, and went out of the room to pin the lacrosse practice notice on the board.

The girls held an informal meeting about the practice, and one and all determined not to turn up. It was Saturday, and, if they wished, they could go for nature-rambles. All the first and second forms decided to do this, even Antoinette, who detested walking.

133

So, to the astonishment of Miss Roberts and Miss Jenks, the whole of the two lowest forms went off in the sunshine together, taking with them nature notebooks and collecting tins and jars, chattering loudly as they passed by the windows of the mistresses' common room.

"*Well!*" said Miss Roberts, looking after the laughing girls, "what's come over them? Why this sudden, violent and wholesale interest in nature? I thought there was to be a match or lacrosse practice or something."

Mirabel turned up on the playing fields at five to three, grim-faced and determined. But nobody else arrived. Mirabel waited till ten past three, and then, rather white, went back to the school. One of the third formers, hardly able to hide her smiles, told her politely that the first and second formers had all gone out for a nature walk.

Then Mirabel knew that she had lost. It had been her will against the wills of the first and second forms, and they had won. They had ignored her orders. They had shown her what they thought of her and her authority. She sat down in her study, feeling dismayed.

She saw a note on the table addressed to her and opened it. It was a formal resignation from Gladys.

> *I wish to resign my post as vice-captain as I feel I cannot be of any use to you.*

> GLADYS

Mirabel threw the note on to the floor. She felt unhappy and bitter. She had been so pleased to be sports captain. She had worked so hard for that position. She had had such high hopes of putting St. Clare's at the very top of the lacrosse and tennis schools. Now the girls had defied her, and even her best friend had deserted her. It was a bitter hour for Mirabel.

The girls came back from their walk, rosy-cheeked and merry. They heard from the third form how Mirabel had gone out alone to the playing field, and had waited there in vain. They also heard that Gladys had resigned as vice-captain and they were pleased.

134

"Good old Gladys," they said. "We always thought it was funny she should back Mirabel up in her unpleasant ways!"

When Mirabel appeared in public at all that week-end the girls carefully turned away from her. "Almost as if I was in quarantine for something beastly!" thought Mirabel, bitterly. The girl was very worried and unhappy, but far too proud to appeal even to Gladys for comfort. Gladys was miserable too, and would have made things up with Mirabel at once if her friend had turned to her, or had admitted that she had been too high-handed with the younger ones. But Mirabel was cold and stand-offish, and gave Gladys no chance to be friendly.

The exam. was to be held the next week, and most of the girls were feeling the strain. Only a few, like clever Pam, or the placid Hilary, did not seem to worry. Felicity was not to take the exam.

A specialist had come from London to see her. He spoke to Miss Theobald very seriously.

"This girl is on the verge of a nervous breakdown," he said. "Her mind seems full of music and nothing but music. See how she plays an imaginary violin, and strains to hear the tune. She must do no more work in music for a year."

Miss Theobald nodded. How she wished Felicity's proud parents had not insisted on their gifted girl working for that difficult music exam! How much better it would have been for her to have dropped her music for a while, and to have entered into the ordinary, normal life of the other fifth formers, instead of losing herself night and day in her beloved music. Now her music might suffer because Felicity's brain had been worked too hard.

"Parents' fault, I suppose?" said the specialist, writing a few notes in his case-book. "Why will parents of gifted children always push them so hard?"

"Just selfishness," said Miss Theobald. "Well – you think we must keep Felicity in bed for a time – then let her get up and wander round a bit, without any lessons – and then gradually join in with the others, without doing any music at all?"

"She can *play* at her music, but not work at it," said the specialist. "Let her enjoy it without worrying about it. She will probably do that anyhow when she knows she is not to work for the music exam. for at least another two years."

Felicity's parents came to see her, worried and dismayed. They remembered how Miss Theobald had pleaded with them not to push Felicity on so quickly. They were frightened when they saw her white face and enormous, dark-rimmed eyes.

"Don't worry too much," said Miss Theobald. "We have stopped her in time. Her sleep-walking gave us warning. Mam'zelle discovered that, and so we have been able to deal with Felicity quickly. Soon she will be a normal, happy girl again, and when she knows she need not work night and day for her music exam., a great weight will be off her mind, and she will laugh and chatter and be as cheerful as the others."

It was a rather subdued father and mother that went home that day. "Miss Theobald might have said, 'I told you so,' to us," said Felicity's mother. "But she didn't. Poor Felicity – I feel we are very much to blame for all this."

The other sleep-walker, Anne-Marie, was not having a very good time. Whenever the first or second formers saw her coming, they immediately put on glassy stares, and with out-stretched hands, began to glide here and there. Anne-Marie hated this teasing, and when it spread to the fifth form too, and glassy eyes appeared there also, Anne-Marie was very near tears.

"It's beastly of you," she said to Alison and Angela, who laughed at her. "I know I shan't pass the exam. if you all jeer at me like this. It's mean of you."

"Well, you're pretty mean yourself," said Alison. "You keep on doing beastly things to *me*, don't you? Where have you put my geometry set you hid last week?"

Anne-Marie stared in surprise. She hadn't the least idea what Alison was talking about.

136

"Oh, don't put on that wide-eyed innocent look," said Alison, impatiently. "We all know you can act, but don't try to take *us* in by it! I know jolly well you're jealous of me because Miss Willcox likes me better than she likes you, and you're trying to get back at me by hiding my things and making silly bits of trouble for me!"

"I'm not," said Anne-Marie, her voice trembling with indignation. "I wouldn't dream of doing such a thing. I haven't *touched* your things! And as for being jealous of you, you needn't worry! I've no time for Miss Willcox now! I'm sure she's not as clever as you think. And what's more I'll show you she isn't."

"Don't be silly," said Alison. "And don't talk about Miss Willcox like that. You're just plain jealous and you're taking my things and being beastly just to get even with me."

"I tell you I'm not playing tricks on you, and I'm not jealous," cried Anne-Marie. "You can keep Miss Willcox all to yourself! I don't ever want to see her again! *Deirdre* Willcox indeed! Her name is Doris, just plain Doris – I saw it written in one of her books. I bet she calls herself Deirdre just because she thinks Doris is too ordinary. She's a – a – silly pretender!"

Anne-Marie flung herself out of the room, and Alison stared after her in rage. Angela laughed.

"You two amuse me," she said. "I'm glad I don't go off the deep end about any one like you do! Silly, I call it!"

"Oh, *do* you!" said Alison, in a cutting voice. "Well, let me tell you, you're just as bad in another way – you smile sweetly at the lower form kids and get them all round you to wait on you – then when you're tired of them, you just tick them off – and they're as miserable as can be. I bet you're partly responsible for Jane Teal trying to run away!"

Angela opened her mouth to answer heatedly, but just then the door opened and Anne-Marie popped her head in again.

"I'll show Miss Doris Willcox up tomorrow, in front of the whole class!" she said. "You see if I don't! Then you'll have to say I'm right, and you'll be jolly sick you didn't see through her. So there!"

The door banged and Anne-Marie disappeared. "I'm tired of Anne-Marie and her silly ways," said Alison, who still thought that it was she who was playing tricks on her, and had no idea it had been Alma. "Let her do what she likes. I shall always like Miss Willcox!"

Anne-Marie Traps Miss Willcox

Anne-Marie had prepared her little trap for Miss Willcox, and she had prepared it very carefully. Every week Miss Willcox set the girls some kind of composition to do, and they sent in their entries, which were carefully gone through by her and marked.

This week the subject set was a poem. It had to be only eight lines long, the first and third lines to rhyme, and the second and fourth, the fifth and seventh and the sixth and eighth. The subject was to be "Thoughts."

The fifth form grumbled. They didn't like writing poetry, they *couldn't* write poetry, it was a silly waste of time for them in exam. week. It was just like Miss Willcox to set a poem for them to do! So they grumbled and groaned, but all the same they managed to produce something that could be called a poem.

Anne-Marie had hunted through the poets for a lesser-known poem that would suit her purpose. If only she could find one that would just do! And by great good fortune she suddenly found exactly what she wanted. It was a little eight-line poem by Matthew Arnold, called "Despondency", which seemed to Anne-Marie to be just what she wanted.

She copied it out in her big, rather sprawly hand-writing. Really it seemed as if it was her own poem, it was just as sad as the ones she liked to write!

Anne-Marie sent the poem in with those of the others of

138

her form. She signed her name at the bottom. Now, Miss Doris Willcox, we will see if you know good poetry when you see it!

The English lesson duly arrived, and Alison glanced curiously at Anne-Marie, who seemed excited. Was she really going to carry out her silly threat and do something to Miss Willcox? Alison felt a little disturbed. Ought she to warn Deirdre?

Miss Willcox arrived, carrying a sheaf of poems in her hand. She looked as soulful as ever, and wore a trailing crimson scarf round her swan-like neck.

The first part of the lesson was given to the reading of a play. Then came the time set apart for the commenting on the girls' own work. Miss Willcox pulled the sheaf of poems towards her.

"Not a very good set," she remarked, slipping the elastic band off the papers. "I suppose the exam. has had an effect on your creative powers. Pam's is the best – quite a praise-worthy little effort, simple and honest. Claudine, I can't pass yours. You may have meant it to be funny, but it isn't."

Claudine made a face, which fortunately for her Miss Willcox did not see. Miss Willcox dealt with every one's poems rapidly, quoting from one or two, praising here and there, and condemning the efforts of Doris, Angela and Carlotta.

Then she came to the last one, which was Anne-Marie's. She looked round the class, a rather spiteful look in her large eyes.

"And now at last we come to the poet of the class, Anne-Marie. A sad, heart-rending poem as usual. Listen to the wailings of our poet.

"THOUGHTS

The thoughts that rain their steady glow,
Like stars on life's cold sea,
Which others know, or say they know –
They never shone for me.

Thoughts light, like gleams, my spirit's sky,
But they will not remain.
They light me once, they hurry by,
And never come again."

Miss Willcox read these lines out in a mock-heroic way, exaggerating the feeling in them, making fun of the whole poem. She put down the paper.

"Anne-Marie, why must you write like this? It is all so silly and insincere and quite meaningless. What for instance can you possibly mean by 'Stars on life's cold sea?' What *is* life's cold sea? Just words that came into your head and you put them down because they sounded grand. Life's cold sea! Ridiculous!"

Anne-Marie stared at Miss Willcox steadily. She felt very triumphant. That wasn't *her* poem! It was written by a great poet, not by Anne-Marie at all! That just showed that Miss Willcox didn't know a thing and wasn't any judge of good poetry!

Miss Willcox didn't like the steady, queerly triumphant look on Anne-Marie's face. She felt a wave of anger against her.

"You have the scansion and the rhyming *quite* correct!" she said scornfully to Anne-Marie, "but all the same I consider your poem the worst of the form."

"Miss Willcox," said Anne-Marie, suddenly, in a high, clear voice, "I'm so sorry – I think I must have made a mistake in sending in that poem! I don't believe it is mine after all!"

The class turned to look at Anne-Marie. She sat tensely, still with that triumphant look on her face.

"What do you mean?" said Miss Willcox, impatiently. "Not *your* poem? Then whose is it? I must say it *sounds* exactly like yours!"

"It's – it's very kind of you to say that," said Anne-Marie, "because you see – that poem is by Matthew Arnold, not by me at all. I'm glad you think his poetry is like mine. I feel honoured. Though I don't suppose, if he

140

were alive, he would be at all pleased to hear the things you have just said about his little poem – it's queer to think you consider *his* poem the worst in the form!"

There was dead silence. Alison turned scarlet, seeing the trap Anne-Marie had set for Miss Willcox, and the prompt way in which she had fallen headlong into it. Anne-Marie pulled a volume of Matthew Arnold's poems from her desk and opened it at a certain page. "Here's the poem," she said, getting up from her desk. "It's called 'Despondency' not 'Thoughts'. I'll show it to you, Miss Willcox."

Miss Willcox had gone white. She knew it had been a trap now – Anne-Marie's revenge for the cruel words she had spoken to her some days back. She had shown her up in front of the whole class. Oh why, why had she said that the poem was the worst in the form? Why had she said such spiteful things? Only to hurt Anne-Marie, and because she thought she wanted taking down two or three pegs.

Alison was terribly distressed. She hated to see Miss Willcox trapped like that – and she also hated to think that the teacher had allowed herself to be trapped because of her own petty spite. She looked with dislike at the triumphant Anne-Marie.

"You have cheated, Anne-Marie," said Miss Willcox, trying to regain her dignity. "I shall have to report you to Miss Theobald for a grave act of deceit."

"Yes, Miss Willcox," said Anne-Marie maliciously, and the English mistress knew that it would be no good reporting Anne-Marie – for Anne-Marie would also report her own side of the matter, and Miss Theobald would not think very much of a teacher who condemned lines by a great poet just because she thought they were written by a school-girl she disliked.

The bell rang, and never did Miss Willcox feel so relieved to hear it. She gathered up her books and sailed out. The girls rounded on Anne-Marie.

"That was a beastly thing to do!" said Hilary.

"I thought it was funny," said Claudine.

141

"You would!" said Pat. "It was certainly clever, but it wasn't a decent thing to do."

"I know it wasn't," said Anne-Marie, defiantly. "But I wanted to get my own back. And I did."

"Well, I hope you're happy about it," said Alison, bitterly. "Trying to humiliate a good teacher in front of the whole class."

"Did she feel sorry for poor little Doris-Deirdre then?" began Anne-Marie, but Hilary was not going to allow any spite of that sort.

"Shut up, both of you," she said. "Maybe you won't be such an ass over Miss Willcox now, Alison – and perhaps, now you've taken your revenge, Anne-Marie, you'll cool off and try to behave decently for the rest of the term. Alison has complained to me about your behaviour to her, and it's got to stop."

"I don't know what you mean by my 'behaviour to Alison'," said Anne-Marie, puzzled. "She complains that I take her things, and play tricks on her, but I don't. Why should I? I'm not jealous of her or anything. She can keep Miss Willcox all to herself if she wants to! *I* don't mind!"

Most of the class, although they thought it was not a nice thing to humiliate a mistress publicly, had secretly enjoyed the excitement. Alma certainly had, for she had often been held up to ridicule by Miss Willcox for her complete inability to appreciate any fine literature at all. She was glad to see her defeated by Anne-Marie – and she was glad too when she heard Alison openly accusing Anne-Marie of the tricks she, Alma, had been playing on the unsuspecting Alison!

"I'll play just one more and that shall be the last," she thought. "I know she had a box of sweets sent to her today. I'll slip in and take those when she isn't there, and she'll blame Anne-Marie again!"

But Alma tried her tricks once too often. When she slipped into Alison's study, it was empty, and she picked up the box of sweets quickly. She hurried to her own study and ran in.

To her dismay both Alison and Angela were there, waiting to ask Pauline something! Alison immediately saw the box of sweets in Alma's hand.

"Those are my sweets!" she said. "You beast, you took them out of my study! Alma, you're a thief! I'm sure you were a thief before too – you pilfered the cupboard outside, when the second formers hid their stuff there. Angela, isn't she absolutely awful?"

Alma stood there stubbornly, trying to think of some way out. "I wasn't going to eat them," she said at last. "I was only playing a trick on you because I don't like you."

"You were stealing," said Alison, furiously. "You know you meant to eat them! This will have to be told to Hilary. It's simply awful for a fifth former to be caught stealing."

Alma sat down suddenly, feeling frightened. She had had a solemn and very serious talking to by Miss Theobald about being found in the cupboard the other night, and it had been impossible to convince the Head Mistress that she had not been doing anything wrong. If this got to her ears, matters would be even more serious.

"I didn't steal them, Alison," she said, desperately. "I tell you, I was just paying you out because you stopped me going to the cupboard where the second formers put their food – though you didn't know it. I took your knitting-needles – and your geometry set – and other things. Only to spite you, though, not to steal them. They're all here, look!"

She unlocked her desk in the corner and before Alison's astonished eyes lay all the things she had missed during the last week or two!

"Bring them into my study," said Alison, completely at a loss to know what to do or say. "I'll have to think about this. What a beast you are, Alma – especially as you knew I was blaming Anne-Marie all the time."

Alma took everything back, weeping. Alison took one look at the puffy, pasty face and turned away in dislike. How could a girl who had been in the top form do things like this? Perhaps that was why she had been dropped back into the fifth – maybe because of some disgrace or other!

A Few Things Are Cleared Up

"Wait till the exams. are over before you make any fuss about Alma," said Angela to Alison. "Oh dear – no wonder Anne-Marie didn't know what we were talking about when we kept accusing her of taking your things!"

"I shall have to apologize to her," said Alison, gloomily. "Blow Alma – what a first-class idiot she is, really! Isn't she queer? I don't understand her at all. Sometimes I think she's daft."

The exams. were now pressing on the girls, and they were working feverishly. Only Pam appeared to find them easy. Hilary worked through her papers methodically, and so did Pat and Isabel, Bobby and Janet, but Carlotta, Claudine and Angela got very hot and bothered. So, queerly enough, did Mirabel, which was unusual for her, but she had given so much of her time to the organizing of the school games that she had not worked as well at her exam. tasks as the others had.

"These awful questions!" she said, as she read one after another. "I can't seem to answer any of them!"

At last the exams. were over and the whole form heaved a sigh of relief. What a week it had been! The girls wanted to yell and laugh and stamp and rush about. They became very boisterous, even the quiet Pam. But the teachers turned a blind eye and a deaf ear on the yelling girls, and did not even appear to see Carlotta doing cartwheels all round the gym.

"Thank goodness we haven't got to wait long for the results," said Doris. "I hate having to wait weeks. Miss Cornwallis says we shall know in a few days."

"How's little Jane Teal?" said Pat, remembering the first former for the first time for a few days. "Is she better?"

"She's over the flu," said Isabel, "but Matron says she's

144

still worried in her mind. When she was so ill, she kept raving about the fire-bell, and Mirabel and Angela. I rather think there's going to be a few inquiries made about certain members of our form soon! Poor Jane – it's rotten to think no one ever owned up about that bell, but let Jane take the blame. It made Mirabel simply beastly to her. She is the only person that hasn't been to see Jane in the san. Did you know?"

"Just like her," said Pat.

The exam. results came out and were posted up on the board. Pam and Hilary were top with honours. The others came in turn down the list. Carlotta was glad to see she had passed. Doris just scraped through too, and so did Claudine and Alison.

Three girls failed. They were Angela, Alma – and, most surprisingly, Mirabel!

Alma had not expected to pass. Angela was amazed that *she* hadn't! As for Mirabel, she was humiliated beyond words. To think that she, sports captain of St. Clare's should have failed. She rushed off to her study, filled with shame and horror. How every one would sneer!

Gladys, who had hardly spoken with Mirabel since she had resigned as vice-captain, stared in amazement at the exam. results. Mirabel failed! She could hardly believe her eyes. With her heart full of sympathy and warmth she hurried off to find her one-time friend.

Mirabel was sitting by the window, her humiliation almost more than she could bear. Gladys went to her, and took her hand.

"Bad luck, old thing," she said. "I'm awfully sorry. You worked too hard at the matches and things, that's all. Don't worry too much about it. Two others have failed as well."

Mirabel was touched by Gladys's warm sympathy. She had felt lonely and deserted. With tears in her eyes she gazed at Gladys, and tried to speak.

"I can't bear it," she said at last. "They'll all laugh at me. Me, the sports captain! They'll be glad to laugh too.

They hate me. Every one hates me. Where have I gone wrong? I mean to do so well."

"Let's be friends again, Mirabel," said Gladys. "You need me, don't you? You wouldn't let me help you at all this term – but let me help you now. The girls don't really hate you – they admired you awfully at the beginning of the term, and there's no reason why they shouldn't again."

Poor Mirabel – and poor Angela! Both liked to shine, and both had failed. What was the use of being sports captain, what was the use of being the most beautiful girl in the school, if your brains were so poor you couldn't even get as good marks as Doris or Alison!

Claudine had been rather quiet for a day or two. She had been to see Jane Teal and taken her a lovely little handkerchief she had embroidered for her. Then she sought out Antoinette and made a proposal to her that surprised that second former very much.

"What! Tell Miss Theobald that I rang the fire-bell!" said Antoinette, in surprise and disgust. "Are you mad, Claudine?"

"Yes, perhaps," said Claudine, thoughtfully. "I am afraid I have caught a little of this English sense of honour, alas! I feel uncomfortable *here* when I think of Jane Teal worrying about the fire-bell, and of Mirabel thinking it is Jane. It is a great pity but I fear I have caught this sense of honour, Antoinette."

"Oh, it is catching?" said Antoinette, in alarm. "I do not want to get it, it is an uncomfortable thing to have. See how it makes you behave, Claudine."

"I will go to Miss Theobald and tell her it was all my fault," said Claudine, at last. "You do not need to come into it, Antoinette. After all, it was my idea, and you only carried it out. I will go and confess."

She gave a huge sigh and went off. Miss Theobald was startled and amused to see Claudine arriving with a saintly and determined expression on her face.

"Miss Theobald, I have caught the sense of honour from somebody at St. Clare's," announced Claudine. "I have
146

come to make a confession. I told my little sister to ring the fire-bell, when Mirabel was about to hold her stupid meeting. I did not mean to own up, but now I feel uncomfortable *here* about it."

Claudine pressed her tummy, and Miss Theobald listened gravely. "I am glad you have owned up, Claudine," she said. "It was a silly thing to do, but it became a serious thing when some one else was suspected of it. Please tell Hilary. I shall not punish Antoinette, but she too must own up to Jane Teal, and put her mind at rest."

Claudine went out, knowing that her real punishment was to be owning up to the serious head-girl of the form. Hilary did not favour misbehaviour of this kind now that they were top-formers, and she had a way of talking that at times made Claudine feel very small. She made her feel small now.

"You don't realize that next term we shall all be in the top form," she said to Claudine. "From there we go out into the world. We can't behave like naughty children in the first form now. We have to set an example to the younger ones, we have to learn what responsibility means!"

"You should be a preacher, Hilary," said Claudine, jokingly.

But Hilary was not in a mood to be joked with. She took her position as head-girl very seriously, all the more so because she knew she would not be head-girl of the sixth. She was only staying one term more, and the head-girl must be some one staying for three terms. Every one was wondering who would be chosen.

Claudine went off, abashed, and found Antoinette, who was highly indignant at being sent off to Jane Teal to confess. But when she saw Jane's face, she was not sorry she had gone.

"Oh," said Jane, "was it really you, Antoinette? Oh, I'm glad you told me. You know, I really began to feel it *might* have been me, I was so worried about it. Whatever will Mirabel say?"

Mirabel soon heard about it. Gladys told her. She flushed uncomfortably, thinking of the hard time she had given poor

Jane because of her unjust suspicions. She thought for a while and then went straight off to the san., where Jane still was.

"Jane, I've heard who rang the fire-bell," said Mirabel, hardly liking to meet Jane's eyes. "It wasn't you, and I was sure it was. I was beastly to you – left you out of matches unfairly – and things like that. I'm – I'm sorry about it. I . . ."

"It's all right, Mirabel," said Jane, eagerly. "I don't mind now. Not a bit. All I want is to get up and practice hard for you again, and perhaps play in a match before the term ends."

Jane's warm response and loyalty were very pleasant to Mirabel, who had been very miserable. She smiled at the first former, left her some barley sugar, and went back to her study, thinking how nice it was to have some one look at her with liking once again.

Mirabel's visit to Jane made a great impression on the lower forms. Jane soon spread it abroad, and spoke so glowingly of Mirabel's kind words to her, that the younger ones began to get over their dislike and defiance. They had deserted the practice field, and had shown little or no interest in games since Mirabel had cancelled their match – but now they gradually drifted back, and Mirabel found, to her delight, that they seemed as keen as ever.

Gladys took back her resignation, and Mirabel set to work humbly and happily to make out games lists again and to arrange matches – but she let Gladys do at least half of it, and was careful to listen to her and to take her advice when she gave it. The two were much happier than they had ever been before and Gladys was glad to see her friend learning from the bad mistakes she had made.

"Looks as if Mirabel will be a good captain after all," said Bobby in surprise. "Well, well – we're all turning over a new leaf! There's Felicity back again, not caring two hoots about her music for a bit, and being quite one of us – and there's Anne-Marie gone all friendly and jolly since Alison apologized to her for suspecting her wrongly – and there's

Alison behaving sensibly too, now that she sees through dear Deirdre – and Angela isn't being such an idiot with the younger ones since she failed in her exam."

"No – that was a shock that pulled her together a bit," said Pat. "She's working hard now. Did you know that Hilary gave her a most awful talking to. She wept buckets of tears, and was furious with Hilary – but she certainly has been better since."

"It's only Alma that's still a pain in the neck," said Isabel. "I hate speaking to her even. I know Hilary's gone to tell Miss Theobald about her taking those things of Alison's. I bet she'll be expelled or something if she isn't careful."

But Alma was not expelled. Instead Hilary explained something to the girls that made them feel rather uncomfortable.

"I told Miss Theobald all about our trouble with Alma," said Hilary, "and she told me we must be patient with her and put up with her, because she can't help it just now. There's something wrong with her glands, that can't be put right for about six months. That's why she's so fat, and always hungry, and looks so pasty and funny. She was sent off from her last school in disgrace – but Miss Theobald wants to keep her here and help her, till she can have some sort of marvellous operation done that can put her right."

"Poor old Pudding," said Doris. "She's her own enemy, I suppose – or her glands are, whatever they may be! Well – I suppose we must put up with our Alma, and grin and bear it when she chews and sucks and gobbles." Doris began to imitate Alma at a meal, and the girls screamed with laughter.

But there was no real unkindness in the laughter. One and all were ready to put up with Alma now and help her, even selfish little Angela, and wild Carlotta. They were growing up, they were fifth formers, they could behave decently. St. Clare's put its mark on you by the time you were in the fifth form!

149

Who Shall Be Head Of The School?

After the exam. the girls relaxed with pleasure and relief. The teachers gave them less prep. to do, and the fifth formers spent pleasant evenings in their own studies or each others', talking and laughing.

"Christmas will soon be upon us," said Pat. "The rest of this term will fly! I always like the Christmas term – it begins in summer-time, when the September sun is still hot, and it often ends in snow, with Christmas beckoning round the corner."

"You sound quite poetic," said Doris. "Anne-Marie used to say things like that!"

Anne-Marie laughed. She had not written any poems for some time, for, after the success of her trick on Miss Willcox, she had felt rather ashamed of herself. After all, *she* had pretended too, just like Miss Willcox, *she* had tried to write poems that sounded very grand, but were quite worthless really. Now Anne-Marie was determined to wait till she had something to say, before she wrote poetry again.

She had had a talk with Miss Theobald, who had heard of Anne-Marie's "cheating" as Miss Willcox called it. The Head Mistress hadn't much time for the English teacher herself, sensing that she was insincere and rather conceited – but she could not allow any of the girls to flout authority, or be insolent, without reprimanding them severely.

So Anne-Marie had had a bad twenty minutes, and had come away a sadder and wiser fifth former, determined that she would write no more "wonderful" poetry until, as Miss Theobald said, she had something real and honest and sincere in her heart to put into her writing and make it worth while.

Mirabel had got over the shock of failing in the exam., and was trying to make the lower forms forget her stupid arrogance and harshness. Her voice was still loud and clear, but not haughty or dictatorial, and she no longer walked as if the whole earth belonged to her. She was a wiser person altogether, and the girls respected her for being able to change herself so completely.

Jane Teal was once again working hard for Mirabel, exulting in her returned health and strength, a great weight off her mind. Angela no longer gave the younger ones so many jobs to do, and she and Alison did their mending together. Hilary had made a great impression on Angela when she had ticked her off, and had really frightened her.

"You're a poor, poor thing, Angela," she had told her. "You use your pretty face and smile to save yourself trouble, and you are getting a lazy mind and a lazy body, letting other people do the things *you* ought to do. No wonder you failed in the exam. – and failed miserably too! If you're not careful you'll go *on* being a failure in all kinds of ways, and people will laugh at you instead of admiring and respecting you. What do you suppose Jane and Sally and Violet and the rest of your lower form slaves think of their darling beautiful Angela now, when they see that she and Alma tied for bottom place in the exam! Pull yourself together a bit, for goodness' sake."

Each term brought different things to learn, besides lessons. Those girls who faced their difficulties, saw and understood their faults, conquered their failings, and became strong characters and leaders would make the finest wives and mothers of the future. Miss Theobald watched the fifth formers carefully, and was proud of many of them.

She remembered them as silly little first formers, and a little less-silly second formers. She remembered Pat and Isabel O'Sullivan, the "stuck-up twins" as they had been called, when they first came. She remembered how Mirabel had vowed not to stay longer than half a term, and had misbehaved herself dreadfully in her first term. She remembered the wildness of Carlotta, who had come to St. Clare's from circus-life, untamed and head-strong.

She remembered Bobby, whose brilliant brains were once

only used in mad and clever tricks – and Claudine, untruthful, deceitful and unscrupulous, who was at last finding
responsibility and a sense of honour. Here were all these
girls now, dependable, honest-minded, hard-working, and
responsible. Truly St. Clare's was a school to be proud of.

Before the end of the term came the Head Mistress must
choose the head-girl for the whole school. All the sixth were
leaving, and the fifth were to go up, with one or two new
girls. Hilary was the only one of the fifth who was not staying on for one more whole year. She was only to stay one
term more, and then she was to go to India to be with her
parents there.

Otherwise Hilary would have been head of the sixth, and
a good responsible head she would have made. But now
some one else must be chosen. The girls wondered who it
would be. It was a tremendous honour, for the head-girl of
the sixth would be the head-girl of the whole school, a
person of great influence.

"It won't be me, anyway," said Doris, comfortably. "I'm
too stupid."

"And it won't be me," said Carlotta. "I'm still too wild."

"Not me," said Bobby, grinning. "I'm still too much
given to playing tricks. Didn't Mam'zelle jump when she
drank her glass of milk this morning and found a black
beetle at the bottom?"

The girls giggled. It was a silly trick, but had caused a lot
of fun. Bobby had popped a little tin black beetle into Mam'-
zelle's glass of mid-morning milk, and her horror when she
had drunk all the milk and then had suddenly seen the beetle
at the bottom had been most amusing to watch.

"*Tiens!*" she had cried. "What is this black animal I
have almost drunk? Oh, la, la, that it should choose my glass
and no one else's!"

The girls recalled all the tricks Bobby and Janet had played
on poor Mam'zelle – the way they had made the plates
dance – the dreadful stink-balls – and many others. They had
all been good fun, and Mam'zelle had always joined in the
laughter afterwards.

152

"We break up in three days' time," said Bobby. "Then heyho for the holidays – and when we come back, we shall all be sixth formers, grave and serious and solemn! No tricks then – no giggles – no messing about!"

"Oh rubbish!" said Carlotta. "We shan't suddenly alter just because we're sixth formers. We shall be just the same. I do wonder who will be head-girl. Perhaps one of the twins will."

"I hope not," said Pat, at once. "I'd hate to be something Isabel wasn't, and she would hate it too. Otherwise we'd either of us love it. It's the thing I'd like best in the world at the moment. I love St. Clare's, and I'm proud of belonging to it. If I could do something for it I would – but I don't want to do something that I can't share with Isabel."

"I feel the same about that," said Isabel. "But if we *did* have the honour of being asked, either of us, to be head-girl, we'd say no. Anyway, there are plenty of others who would make better head-girls than we should."

At that very moment the matter was being decided by Miss Theobald, Miss Cornwallis and Mam'zelle. They were sitting together in the Head's drawing-room, discussing the very weighty and important question of who should be the next head-girl. It was important because the head-girl had a powerful influence on the whole school, and was, in fact, typical of the spirit of St. Clare's.

They were going down the list of girls. "Hilary can't be, of course," said Miss Cornwallis. "A pity, because she has had great experience of being head-girl in three or four forms. Still, perhaps it is time some one else had a chance of showing leadership."

"Janet?" said Miss Theobald.

The others shook their heads. Janet could still be hot-tempered and wilful at times. She had not yet learnt to guard her sharp tongue completely. A head-girl had to have complete control of herself.

"Not Bobby, of course," said Miss Cornwallis. "Brilliant, trustable, but still a little unsteady. What about Gladys?"

"Too gentle – not enough of a leader," said Miss Theobald, who knew the characters of every girl in a most remarkable way. "And Claudine I am afraid we must also cross out, Mam'zelle."

Mam'zelle sighed. It had been a secret wish with her for two or three terms that Claudine, her little Claudine, might be head of St. Clare's, the school in which Mam'zelle had taught for so many many years. But even Mam'zelle, biassed as she was, knew that Claudine was not fit to lead the others.

"If she had been at St. Clare's when she was thirteen now," said Mam'zelle, "ah, then my little Claudine might have had time to learn enough to become head-girl!"

Both Miss Theobald and Miss Cornwallis had their doubts about this. In fact, Miss Cornwallis thought that if Claudine had been at St. Clare's ever since she was a baby, she would still not have been suitable for a head-girl. But neither wanted to upset Mam'zelle, who adored her two nieces, so they said nothing.

"Alma, certainly not, poor girl," said Miss Theobald. "She is a most unfortunate child. Perhaps when she is in really good health, she will improve. Carlotta now – no, I think not. Still rather unaccountable and uncontrolled in her temper. I always feel she is still capable of slapping people if she doesn't approve of them."

Mam'zelle remembered various slapping episodes in Carlotta's school-life and smiled. "Ah, she would slap the first formers hard if they did not behave!" she said. "She would be an amusing head-girl, but perhaps not a very good one."

"Felicity, no," said Miss Cornwallis. "She will always be apt to forget everything when her music fills her mind. She will perhaps someday be one of the foremost musicians or composers, but only in her art will she be fit to lead others."

"Angela and Alison – neither of them leaders in any way," said Miss Theobald. "How good it would be for both of them to he head-girls, and feel the weight of leadership and responsibility on their shoulders – but how bad for the school! Alison is still such a feather-head, and Angela has

154

a lot to learn yet. Three more terms to learn it in – well, maybe it will be enough."

"Anne-Marie would be hopeless," said Mam'zelle, "so would Pauline."

"That leaves Doris, Pam and the twins," said Miss Theobald, looking at her list.

"Doris is too stupid," said Mam'zelle. "Still she cannot roll her 'R's' for me in the French way. Ah, she will be a great success on the stage, that girl, she is so clever a mimic. But she is stupid in all other ways, though a nice, nice girl."

The others agreed. "Pam would make an ideal head-girl," said Miss Theobald, "but she is too young. Almost two years younger than the oldest in the fifth. She is staying on two years, so perhaps she will be head-girl in the future. A nice, hard-working, quiet and dependable child."

"That only leaves the O'Sullivan twins," said Miss Cornwallis, "and I am sure that we cannot choose one without the other. They are inseparable and always have been. The other twin would feel very much left out if we chose one of them."

"Ah – I have it!" said Mam'zelle, suddenly, banging the table and making the other mistresses jump. "I have it! Yes, we will have *two* head-girls! Why not? Is not St. Clare's bigger than ever it was? Has not the head-girl more than enough to do? Then we will have *two* head-girls, girls who will work together as one – so why not the O'Sullivan twins?"

Miss Theobald and Miss Cornwallis looked at each other. It was a good idea. Two head-girls who were twins would certainly work very well together, and could share the responsibility well. Pat and Isabel had consistently done good work, and had grown into splendid, trustworthy and sensible girls.

"Yes," said Miss Theobald, at last. "It's a very good idea indeed. The twins will make fine head-girls. It will do them a world of good, for they have never undertaken any kind of leadership here so far. They shall be joint head-girls. I will make the announcement tomorrow."

So, when the whole school was called together for the head to announce the changes in the coming term, the names of the two head-girls were given.

"We have carefully studied the question of who shall be head-girl of the school for the coming year," said Miss Theobald. "And I think there is no doubt that our choice is wise and will be very popular. St. Clare's is growing fast, and the head-girl has a great deal to do; sometimes too much. So we have decided to have *two* head-girls working together, and we have chosen a pair who have been with us from the first form, and have made their way up the school steadily and well, winning every one's respect and admiration. Next term the O'Sullivan twins will be our head-girls!"

There was a terrific out-burst of cheering, clapping and stamping at these words. Everyone knew the like-as-pea twins, everyone liked them and trusted them. Now they were to be head-girls together – splendid!

The twins were overwhelmed. They blushed scarlet, and when they heard the outburst of cheering, they felt sudden tears pricking their eye-lids. It was a wonderful moment for them. To be chosen to head the school, to lead it, to hold the biggest honour St. Clare's had to offer – that was something worth while.

"Thank you," said Pat, standing up with Isabel, when the cheering had lessened. "We'll – we'll do our very best!"

So they will – and their best will be very good indeed. And there we must leave them, about to have their dearest wish, head-girls of St. Clare's, the finest school they know.

Enid Blyton is Granada's bestselling children's author. Her books have sold millions of copies throughout the world and have delighted children of many nations. Here is a list of her books available from Granada.

First Term at Malory Towers	95p	☐
Second Form at Malory Towers	95p	☐
Third Year at Malory Towers	95p	☐
Upper Fourth at Malory Towers	95p	☐
In the Fifth at Malory Towers	95p	☐
Last Term at Malory Towers	95p	☐
Malory Towers Gift Set	£5.50	☐
The Twins at St Clare's	95p	☐
The O'Sullivan Twins	95p	☐
Summer Term at St Clare's	95p	☐
Second Form at St Clare's	95p	☐
Claudine at St Clare's	95p	☐
Fifth Formers at St Clare's	95p	☐
St Clare's Gift Set	£5.50	☐
Mystery of the Banshee Towers	95p	☐
Mystery of the Burnt Cottage	95p	☐
Mystery of the Disappearing Cat	95p	☐
Mystery of the Hidden House	95p	☐
Mystery of Holly Lane	95p	☐
Mystery of the Invisible Thief	95p	☐
Mystery of the Missing Man	95p	☐
Mystery of the Missing Necklace	95p	☐
Mystery of the Pantomime Cat	95p	☐
Mystery of the Secret Room	95p	☐
Mystery of the Spiteful Letters	95p	☐
Mystery of the Strange Bundle	95p	☐
Mystery of the Strange Messages	95p	☐
Mystery of Tally-Ho Cottage	95p	☐
Mystery of the Vanished Prince	95p	☐

Fiction from Granada in paperback.

Holly Hobbie   Richard Dubleman   £1.25 ☐
The exciting adventures of Liz Dutton who, with her magical friend
Holly Hobbie, wrestles with the dangers of the Guatemalan jungle to
save her father.

Ivory City   Marcus Crouch   95p ☐
A collection of Indian folk tales.

The Trumpeter of Krakov   Agnes Szudek   85p ☐
A collection of Polish folk tales.

War of the Computers   Granville Wilson   85p ☐
A.D. 2010 and a global war breaks out between the computers which
govern Earth.
The Terror Cubes   85p ☐
A.D. 2050 and renegade robots threaten to take over Mankind's
society.

Trebizon Series   Anne Digby
First Term at Trebizon   85p ☐
Second Term at Trebizon   95p ☐
Summer Term at Trebizon   85p ☐
Boy Trouble at Trebizon   95p ☐
More Trouble at Trebizon   85p ☐
The Tennis Term at Trebizon   85p ☐
Summer Camp at Trebizon   95p ☐
Into the Fourth at Trebizon   95p ☐
An exciting new modern school series about Rebecca Mason and
her five friends at boarding school.

The Big Swim of the Summer   Anne Digby   60p ☐
Sara seems all set to win the big swimming race until she gets
involved with the strange new girl at Hocking School.

Bambi's Children Part One   Felix Salten   60p ☐
Bambi's Children Part Two   60p ☐
Fifteen Rabbits   65p ☐
Three books of classic and much loved animal stories.

Shadows in the Pit   Robin Chambers   70p ☐
A tense and exciting science fiction adventure.

Fiction for Younger Readers from Granada in paperback.

McGurk Series E. W. Hildick
Funny and fast moving adventures of boy detective McGurk, head of
the McGurk detective agency, and his friends—Nose, Brains
Bellingham, Joey and Wanda.

The Nose Knows	50p	☐
Deadline for McGurk	50p	☐
The Case of the Condemned Cat	50p	☐
The Menaced Midget	50p	☐
The Case of the Nervous Newsboy	70p	☐
The Great Rabbit Robbery	70p	☐
The Case of the Secret Scribbler	75p	☐
The Case of the Invisible Dog	75p	☐

Grasshopper and the Unwise Owl Jim Slater	75p	☐
Grasshopper and the Pickle Factory	95p	☐

Two stories of a boy who can shrink to six centimetres tall and of the
adventures he has with the animals.

Vlad the Drac Ann Jungman   85p ☐
The adventures of a pint sized vegetarian vampire smuggled into
England from Romania.

Eggbox Brontosaurus Michael Denton   85p ☐
Prince Rudi plans to build a dinosaur from 250,000 eggboxes but to
find this many he has to go on a dangerous and exciting quest,
accompanied only by Ambiguous Dogsbody, his faithful page.

Happy Endings Wendy Craig   85p ☐
A collection of bed-time stories for the very young.

The Princess and the Unicorn Marika Hanbury Tenison £1.25☐
The age old myth beautifully retold and illustrated in colour.

The Short Voyage of the Albert Ross Jan Mark   85p ☐
A sensitive story of the relationship between Steven, who is quiet and
gentle and John, who is boisterous and a bully.

All these books are available at your local bookshop or newsagent, and can be ordered direct from the publisher.

To order direct from the publisher just tick the titles you want and fill in the form below:

Name _____

Address _____

_____

Send to:
Granada Cash Sales
PO Box 11, Falmouth, Cornwall TR10 9EN

Please enclose remittance to the value of the cover price plus:

UK 45p for the first book, 20p for the second book plus 14p per copy for each additional book ordered to a maximum charge of £1.63.

BFPO and Eire 45p for the first book, 20p for the second book plus 14p per copy for the next 7 books, thereafter 8p per book.

Overseas 75p for the first book and 21p for each additional book.

Granada Publishing reserve the right to show new retail prices on covers, which may differ from those previously advertised in the text or elsewhere.